SOTERIA
--
THE BALLOT WARS

A novella by
Joe Gribble

Copyright

Soteria – The Ballot Wars, a novella by Joe Gribble based on the screenplay by the same name.

Copyright © 2023 all rights reserved. No part of this book may be used or reproduced by any means, graphic, electronic, or mechanical, including photocopying, recording, taping, or by any information storage retrieval system without the written permission of Joe Gribble, except in the case of brief quotations embodied in critical articles and reviews.

This book is a work of fiction. The characters, incidents, and dialogue are drawn from the author's imagination and are not to be construed as real. Any resemblance to actual events or persons, alive or dead, is entirely coincidental. Registered trademarks and service marks are the property of their respective owners.

Cover photo cover was designed using assets from Freepik.com.
Library Cataloging Data
Names: Gribble, Joe (Joe Gribble)
Title: *Soteria – The Ballot Wars* / Joe Gribble
6.0 in. x 9.0 in.

Summary: Gabby Hernandez, a military veteran, finds herself thrust into a treacherous web of conspiracy orchestrated by a global syndicate of power-hungry bankers and influential politicians. Hunted relentlessly by the cabal's ruthless assassins, Gabby races against time to bring down the clandestine empire, setting the stage for a pulse-pounding showdown where survival and justice hang by a razor-thin thread.

1. Election Fraud 2. Conspiracy 3. International Cabal 4. Syndicate 5. Political 6. Military 7. Intrigue

SOTERIA
--
THE BALLOT WARS

A novella by
Joe Gribble

Acknowledgements

I would be remiss if I did not acknowledge my wife, Nedra, for her kindness and support as I pursue my 'retirement' projects - writing and volunteering with Team Rubicon, both of which take so much time away from our lives together. She has stood by my side as I lived my career in the US Air Force, maintaining the home front while I was away so many times. She continues to support my volunteer journeys to assist in helping communities recover from disasters, and lets me retreat to my office to write the many screenplays and novels I want to put to paper. She has always truly been the 'iron major' who keeps things running when I am away. She was also kind enough to read through this novella and highlight all the errors in both grammar and plot, making this story much better than it otherwise would have been.

"Those who cast the votes decide nothing.

Those who count the votes decide everything."

Attributed to Josef Stalin

The Ballot Wars

A crowd of people flowed into the lobby of the Willis Tower, their Monday morning enthusiasm in short supply. Their primary goal was to clock in, endure the workday, and return home. Most clutched paper cups filled with coffee, while a few old-timers carried folded newspapers under their arms. The elevator queues stretched on endlessly. Many waiting in the lines hopped on their phones during this downtime to jumpstart their workday, their voices raised to overcome the lobby's clamor, forming an indistinct hum.

At the security checkpoint, another lengthy line snaked far back. Most of the people in this queue had simply forgotten their security badges, their impatience palpable as they waited to obtain temporary passes. However, an unexpected snag clogged the front of the line.

Behind a formidable counter sat a young security guard, his nametag read 'Jones'. Behind him hung a conspicuous sign:

International Banking Institute

Jones scrutinized a set of credentials, comparing the photo to the eccentric man standing before him. He raised an eyebrow at the visitor. "Your name's Gonzo? Seriously?"

Gonzo, the culprit causing the holdup, was in his late twenties. He sported a porn-star mustache and long, jet-black hair. He shrugged, then pointed to his name emblazoned on his fuchsia-colored golf shirt. "So it says."

Jones shook his head. "There's nothin' on the schedule."

"Come on, man. Speed it up!" a voice from further back in the line impatiently urged.

Jones craned his neck, casting a stern glance at the disruptor.

Unfazed, Gonzo removed his backpack, rummaged through a pouch until he retrieved a slip of paper, which he handed over to Jones. "Here's the email. I'm here to troubleshoot your 'NAS'."

Jones took the paper and examined it. "Never heard of a 'NAS'."

Gonzo smiled, exposing his yellowed, coffee-stained teeth. "Network Attached Storage. Maybe you can contact..." Gonzo leaned closer, peering at the paper clutched in Jones's hand. "Mr. Haynes. He's the guy who sent the request."

Jones looked up at Gonzo. "Chief of Security Haynes?" Jones asked. He then grabbed the desk phone: "Yeah, I think I will." He punched in a single number.

In a room furnished with sleek metal desks and an array of computers, a lone phone rang among the silent machines. A very realistic, computer-generated voice answered in a gruff tone, "What?"

Jones's voice emanated from the speaker: "Mr. Haynes, this is officer Jones at reception. I have a technician here from Storage Solutions, but there's nothing on the schedule. Do...."

The computer-generated voice cut Jones off mid-sentence, its tone even gruffer: "Last minute issue with our video security. The CEO complained. Let him in."

Jones's face registered surprise when the phone abruptly disconnected. He gazed up from the phone at Gonzo before returning the handset. Without saying a word he opened a drawer and fished out a badge. He entered some information into his computer, then finally handed the badge to Gonzo: "You'll need an escort."

Gonzo followed his escort, a middle-aged man wearing an ill-fitting suit, out of the service elevator and into a hallway on the fifty seventh floor. Gonzo could tell the man was fit, simply from the way he carried himself. His poorly fitting suit didn't conceal the sidearm his escort carried in a shoulder holster.

They stopped at one of the many doors in the hallway. The escort scanned his badge, then keyed in a code. He opened the door and automatic lights flicked on.

Gonzo followed him inside.

"Welcome to geek heaven," the escort said. "Do your thing. I'll be here at the door if you need me."

The room was, indeed, a geek's dream. Racks and racks of electronics, connected with bundles of cables and fiber. Gonzo walked up and down the aisles of electronics racks until he found what he was looking for. He pulled a slide-out table from the electronics rack, then dug a small laptop from his backpack and placed it on the table. He plugged a wire into one of the laptop ports and connected the other end into a port on the electronics rack.

Gonzo glanced back over his shoulder. His escort stood near the door, checking something on his phone. Gonzo smiled. He made sure his laptop was situated so the escort couldn't see what he was doing. That only left a single security camera that could see down the aisle. Gonzo stepped between the laptop and the security camera, blocking its view, then began typing on his laptop. He hit enter and an upload sequence began – the countdown bar on his screen showed rapid progress.

Buck Winston, mid-60s, sat behind an ornate desk in his corner office, smoldering cigar clenched between his teeth. The windows provided a terrific view of the Chicago skyline, most of it well below Winston's high-rise office on the eighty-fifth floor.

Across from his desk stood Andre, late-40s, tall, with dark, sunken eyes. Andre opened a brown folder, pulled out an 8 by 10 photograph and slapped it down on Buck's desk.

The picture was of a young man wearing an US Air Force uniform. The man in the picture had a hint of Gonzo's facial structure, but no mustache. His hair was military length.

"This is the guy who's been poking at your voting system," Andre said.

Buck looked up at Andre. "You're sure?"

"Certain," Andre said. "Name's Darek Hamlin. He's former Air Force, one tour in Afghanistan."

"He an operator?" Buck asked.

"Hardly," Andre answered. "He was in intelligence, just a code monkey."

Buck rolled the cigar from one side of his mouth to the other. "Dumbass. Probably doesn't even know what he stumbled onto."

Andre left the photo in front of Buck, and slouched down in a chair across from the desk. "How hard do we lean on him?"

Buck took the cigar out of his mouth and rolled it in his fingers. "Hard enough to get his attention." Buck handed the photo back to Andre.

Andre stood and took the photo, sliding it back into the folder. He nodded at Buck and turned to leave through a side door to Buck's office.

"Andre," Buck stopped him.

Andre paused and turned back to face Buck.

"No fingerprints!" Buck said.

"Of course."

Gabby Hernandez, a twenty-three-year-old marketing student, stood next to the street in front of the University of Cincinnati, waiting. She carried a camo-colored backpack slung off one shoulder. It bore a US ARMY label, a nametape - Hernandez - and a patch symbolizing a knight's helmet, a sword, and a lightning flash. She wore her usual cargo pants, a sweater, and worn combat boots.

She checked her watch just as a beat-up car stopped at the curb. Right on time. She would have expected nothing less. Gabby opened the door and climbed in, tossing her backpack into the back seat where it landed next to a nearly identical one.

Darek, hair much longer than in the picture Andre had shown Buck Sexton, welcomed her from the driver's seat. "Hey Gabs. Still carrying our backpack?"

They leaned toward each other and Gabby gave Darek a quick kiss on the cheek.

"Of course," Gabby said as she settled back into her seat and pulled her seat belt on. "It's been a while."

"Too long. I'm sorry," Darek said, fondly looking at his passenger. "That's on me."

Gabby shrugged. "Your text was a nice surprise. I've been wondering what you've been up to."

She could tell Darek was a little uncomfortable.

"Oh, you know. Same old, same old," Darek said.

Same mysterious Darek. Nothing had changed. They locked eyes, neither speaking.

"How's school?" Darek finally asked, breaking the awkward silence.

"Boring," Gabby answered.

"Nothing like the good old days, huh?" Darek asked.

"Ain't that the truth."

Darek dropped the little car into gear and coaxed it away from the curb and into the street. "You ready for a romantic evening?"

Gabby couldn't help but laugh. "Romantic? You? That would be a change."

"You never know," Darek said.

"I'm not really dressed for romantic," Gabby said.

Darek glanced over at her. "I don't know. Your boots just ooze intimacy."

Gabby laughed. "Intimate? Hate to burst your bubble, but that ship sailed a long time ago."

"Yeah, I know. A guy can dream, though. Can't he?"

Darek pulled onto the highway.

They rode in silence for a few minutes. Gabby glanced over at Darek, her voice soft: "How's the leg?"

Darek glanced back at her, then back to the road. He reached down and tapped his knuckles on his lower leg. The knocking sound it made was solid. "Good as ever."

Darek flipped on the CD player. Techno music blasted from the speakers. "Here's the latest riff."

Gabby bounced her head with the rhythm. "I can't believe you're making a living with your music. That's so cool."

Darek looked sideways at Gabby and smiled.

Darek drove downtown, and parked on a street filled with bars and nightclubs.

"It's just this way," he told Gabby, leading her down the street.

A neon sign greeted Gabby and Darek to the "WILD AXE THROWING BAR". The double doors leading inside had small axes for handles. Darek pulled the door open for Gabby. "You're gonna' love this."

Gabby walked inside, not sure what to expect. She was greeted by low, thumping music, interrupted every few seconds by raucous yells from groups of people at the axe throwing lines. The patrons were huddled in small groups facing twenty-foot alleys where axes flew through the air at thick slices of wood, somewhat mutilated by the beating they had received from previous throws. "Holy shit," was all Gabby could think of to say.

"Cool, huh?" Darek said as he stepped in front of her.

Darek led her to the bar, where he had a short conversation with the bartender.

The bartender pointed at one of the unoccupied throwing alleys, then popped the top on a couple of bottled beers and handed them to Darek.

"This way," Darek said, loudly enough to be heard above the noise of the bar. He handed one of the beers to Gabby.

Gabby took a swig from the beer Darek offered and followed, amazed at the variety of people throwing axes. And drinking. She pondered the potential and summed it up as '*an ugly accident waiting to happen'*.

Darek led her to the empty alley.

The floor was covered with straw and sawdust. The alley, from the throwing line to the target, was separated from the adjacent alleys with floor to ceiling plexiglass – for safety Gabby assumed. On their left were several young men wearing suits who appeared to be serious in their axe throwing attempts. On their right were three big men, all with long beards and wearing flannel shirts, and a couple of women wearing sun dresses. Dozens of beer bottles littered a barrel that served as a table.

Darek put his beer on the barrel in their lane, then took a small throwing axe from another, cut-open barrel near the table. "All you have to do," Darek said, "is stand behind this line…". He looked down, then used his good leg to scrape a bunch of sawdust off of a white line painted on the floor. "And aim for the bull's-eye. Darek held his axe back over his right ear, balanced himself, took aim, and flung the small throwing axe toward the wood target. It landed in the third ring. "Easy."

"Easy. Right," Gabby said. She took one of the small throwing axes and stepped up to the line. Mimicking Darek's moves, she exhaled as she launched the axe at the wood block. The axe spun a couple of times in the air and hit the outer edge of the target before bouncing away. She shook her head and took a swig from her beer. "Harder than I thought."

"You'll get it. Just takes a little practice.

Darek took a small throwing axe from the storage barrel and stepped up to the line. "Take your time. Slow is smooth…" He flung the axe forward, striking the second circle from the center. "Smooth is straight."

They played for several minutes. Darek always seemed to hit close to the second ring. Gabby was lucky to even get her little axe to impale itself into the target – usually her throws just hit the target and bounced off.

The server brought them another round of beers.

One of the big, flannel wearing, bearded men in the lane next to them, well on his way to being totally drunk, stepped over and got into Gabby's space. "Come on over here little lady, and I'll show you how it's done." Drunk with courage, he grabbed Gabby's arm.

Gabby recoiled and tried to get out of his grip. She couldn't, so she pushed back - forcefully.

Flannel laughed and pulled Gabby toward the other lane.

Darek finished his throw and turned around in time to see what was happening: "Back off, asshole!" he yelled.

Flannel, his face red, turned his attention to Darek.

Both men stepped toward each other.

Gabby tried to intervene: "Hey, hey. Easy, guys."

The two men went face to face.

Darek had to look up at Flannel, a good six inches taller, but Darek didn't flinch.

Gabby forced herself between them. "No need for this."

Flannel stared at Darek, but talked sideways to Gabby: "I'm gonna' show your little boyfriend how to throw an ax."

Darek grinned. "Here's a thought. One throw each. Loser buys drinks for the other team."

Darek, don't..." Gabby said.

Flannel grinned and nodded. "Done!"

Flannel shoved Darek back, then took a large axe from the barrel and stepped to the throwing line. Holding the axe with both hands, he pulled it way back over his head. With a loud grunt he flipped it over his head and forward. It spun in the air twice and slammed into the target. The axe landed in the first ring outside the center.

Darek took one of the smaller throwing axes out of the barrel and stepped up to the line. "Pretty good, big guy. Now watch how it's done." Darek made one practice swing, then flipped the axe forward. It spun end over end, then landed with a loud smack right in the center of the bullseye.

Flannel growled, then lunged for Darek.

Darek easily ducked and sidestepped the bigger man, then used the beast's momentum against him. With his good leg, Darek tripped Flannel and pushed him to the ground.

Darek quickly jumped on top of Flannel and twisted his arm back up and around, forcefully pinning him to the ground.

Flannel wasn't about to be whipped so easily. He flailed and used his free arm to push himself up off the ground. He tried hard to throw Darek off.

Darek struggled to keep the bigger man down. He kept the big man's arm pinned behind him, and used his good leg to keep Flannel from getting his feet back under him.

Gabby grabbed the big man's leg to help Darek. The big guy was strong, but Gabby was used to being up against much bigger people – mostly men. She glanced back and saw Flannel's lumberjack friends were headed for them. "Darek..." she tried to warn.

Just in time, two big bouncers arrived. They pushed Gabby back and jumped on top of the squabble. They quickly broke up the fight and pulled the two men apart. One bouncer on each man, they yanked them to their feet and forcefully ushered Flannel, and Darek to the door. Gabby followed.

The bouncers followed the two groups outside the bar and stood between them until each group turned to go their separate ways.

Darek and Gabby headed back to Darek's car.

Gabby walked alongside Darek, glancing back every few steps to make sure Flannel and his crew weren't coming for them. She grinned at Darek: "Good move back there."

Darek shook his head. "Bad leg and all, huh? Listen, sorry about that. Last time I was here it was a lot of fun. Guess the bottom-feeders found out about it."

Darek's phone buzzed and he checked it. "Aw shit. Come on..."

He jogged, slightly limping, toward his car.

Gabby hurried to catch up. "What?"

Darek unlocked his door. "It's my house alarm."

Darek drove quickly, and in only minutes they were headed into a small suburban area. He pulled into his driveway.

In the light from the street lamp, Gabby saw Darek's front door was hanging from its hinges, partially open, its glass pane shattered. Several lights were on inside the house. "We should call the cops."

Darek killed the engine and grabbed his door handle. "No cops." He climbed out of the car.

Gabby opened her door and followed Darek up the walkway to his house. "Why no cops?"

Darek carefully opened the front door the rest of the way, but a large sliver of the broken window fell and crashed to the sidewalk, shattering. "Careful of the glass," he said, as he cautiously stepped over the fragments.

Gabby followed Darek in, noting that he didn't answer her question.

Inside, Darek's house was completely trashed. Furniture had been tossed and mutilated, what few plants that were there had been upended, dirt scattered across the carpet.

Gabby quickly glanced around, but Darek seemed to ignore the damage and hurried to a room off the main hallway. Gabby followed.

The door to that room had a cipher lock on the door, but it hadn't held. The door limply hung from its hinges. Gabby helped Darek force the door open, pushing litter on the floor out of the way.

Gabby drew her breath when she got inside. A dozen or so computers and monitors, smashed beyond repair, sat in broken piles on a large desk that butted up against three walls. She watched as Darek picked up a framed image from the floor. Its glass shattered, the frame held a line drawing of a woman wearing a laurel wreath as a crown, below her image was the description: "**Soteria – Goddess of Safety and Preservation**". Darek placed the picture on a table, next to a broken mannequin head wearing a ratty, black wig and a porn star mustache.

"What the hell's going on, Darek?"

Darek just shook his head and stepped back out of the room.

Gabby glanced around before following him out. She hurried past him so she could look him in the eye. "You're back in the business, aren't you?"

Darek stopped. He gently put his hands on Gabby's shoulders and looked at her caringly. "I was never out of the business, Gabs. Just different handlers now."

Gabby shook her head. "I should have known. No way the music was paying your bills."

Darek laughed. "The music's doing quite well. Trust me. It would pay the bills fine."

"Not funny, Darek. The business almost got you killed last time. Your leg..."

"Yeah, but you take a risk every time you cross the street. What I'm doing now, this 'business', it's important. The guys I'm working with... Let's just say they really have a sharp focus on where the threats are – not like last time. You'd get it, I know you would."

"Maybe. I just don't want you to get hurt."

Darek grinned. "I won't. Promise. But right now we have to get out of here. He headed out the front door, with Gabby following. "I've obviously hit a nerve. I'll take you home."

Darek punched a number into his phone and put it to his ear. "I've had uninvited visitors. Need my place tidied up. I'll be at the backup."

It was an awkward, quiet drive to Gabby's apartment building.

Darek broke the silence when he pulled to a stop along the curb. "I'm really sorry about tonight. It wasn't quite the reunion I had planned."

Gabby reached over and took Darek's hand in hers. "I'm not sure what you're up to, what you've gotten yourself into, but please be careful."

Darek squeezed her hand. "I'm fine, really."

"That mess back at your house – that didn't look fine." Gabby looked away, paused a few seconds. She looked back at him: "You know we have your back if you need help."

Darek smiled back at her. "I know. I may take you up on that if I need to. I think I'll have to be offline for a while, though. I'll call you as soon as I can. Don't worry about me."

Gabby leaned in to hug him, then, hesitantly, she grabbed her backpack out of the back seat and climbed out. "In spite of all that happened, it was really good to see you again."

She closed the door and stepped back. Darek waved, then pulled away.

-----SIX MONTHS LATER-----

Gabby stepped off the city bus and slung her backpack over her shoulder. It was Saturday, and the streets were nearly empty. She headed for a two-story office building.

As she approached the floor-to-glass windows at the front of the building she saw a reflection – Darek – at least it looked like him. She watched as the man in the image turned and walked away. Gabby turned and looked behind her, searching for her friend. Nothing. She shook her head. *Just like something he'd do.* It had been six months since she had seen Darek, the night some people had ransacked his house. She had only received texts from him since, assuring her he was all right. He had even hooked her up with this gig when she told him her finances were getting tight.

She shrugged and continued to the door. Gabby pulled her backpack from her shoulder and dug out a badge, held her pass against the sensor, then pushed the door open and stepped inside.

The front lobby was fancy, but dated. She stepped over to the reception desk. "Good morning, Henry."

The guard, in his late forties, monitored the security cameras. He looked up and smiled. A sign behind him read:

STATE BOARD OF ELECTIONS

Gabby looped her badge lanyard over her head.

Henry stood, pushing his wheeled chair back. "Hi Gabby. I figured you'd be working this weekend."

"Looks like you and me both. They're pushing for a clean report before the elections on Tuesday."

"I sure hope we don't have a disaster like the last election."

"That's what we're working on. Gotta' love coming in on Saturdays, though, huh? Hey, how's Danny doing?"

"Better. Should be out of the hospital tomorrow. Thanks for asking."

"Awesome. I told you he'd be fine." Gabby reached out to put her hand on Henry's. "Tell him 'Hi' for me."

Henry nodded.

She smiled and headed to the elevator.

At the elevator, Gabby put her badge up to the sensor and the elevator doors opened. Inside, she pushed the button for the second (top) floor.

Her phone buzzed as she stepped off the elevator. She tapped the voice-mail icon. A missed call from Darek. She smiled and hit 'play'.

I have a new riff for you. Would love your feedback. It's kind of big - just plug your phone into a computer and I'll push it to you over the internet.

Gabby frowned, but dug her phone cord out of her backpack as she walked past several closed office doors before coming to the office where she worked. It was unique, with glass windows framing the top half of the entire hallway wall. She stopped at the door, also with glass at the top, with the stenciled words:

Software Validation - Tabulation

Gabby waved her badge at the sensor, pushed the door open, and stepped inside.

The overhead lights were turned down, dimly lighting the room. A dozen large desks, each with a computer and a pair of monitors, sat in rows. Several evenly spaced concrete pillars kept the ceiling aloft in the large room.

Samar, wearing headphones, was the only other person in the room. He sat behind one of the computers. "Gabby. Good morning," he said when he saw her. He waved at one of the other computer desks. "Your throne awaits."

Gabby pulled her backpack off and slid it beside the chair at the desk next to his. "You're working on Nasira's birthday?"

"Ah, yes. It is unfortunate indeed." He shrugged "However, bills must be paid."

"Don't I know that."

Gabby pulled on a headset and sat down at the computer. She plugged her phone cable into the computer

Samar frowned and shook his head. "It is against the discipline to connect your phone."

"I know. Just need a little power bump. It'll be fine. No one will know."

Samar turned back to his computer, still shaking his head.

Gabby flipped open a notebook on her desk and turned to a marked section. She read the short text, then began typing into the computer. One monitor mimicked her input, and the other monitor displayed "Tabulation statistics". She touched both screens, comparing values.

She didn't notice a message that briefly flashed on her phone: "Downloading", then went away.

The mostly darkened network operations center had a dozen computers on individual desks, each with a bank of large monitors. The ops center was fully staffed, even on a Saturday. A mega-monitor that covered the room's entire front wall displayed a global map. Thousands of yellow dots across the United States were connected with green lines. A few scattered red dots also littered the big map.

A blaring alarm sounded and the heads of the operators all popped up.simultaneously. A bright red icon flashing on the map over southwest Ohio had their attention.

A supervisor, sitting in a command console in the back of the room, quickly stood. He spoke into his headset. "Report!"

The Midwest Region Operator responded: "Breach to the main firewall."

"Isolate and track," ordered the supervisor.

The operator's fingers flew across his keyboard.

The map on the front wall shifted and expanded. A region centered on Ohio came into focus. A thin red line briefly pointed north from the breach location, then disappeared.

The operator's head popped up to glance at the map. "Shit. A little help?"

Two other operators weighed in, fingers rapidly typing.

Multiple red lines suddenly appeared on the map, only to disappear just as quickly.

"Fuck." The operator looked up at the supervisor. "It's not a random attack. They're targeting our system."

"Isolate the attack! Kill it!" the supervisor ordered. He took a landline phone with a red stripe around it out of a similarly red box. He punched '6' then looked up. "Get me a damage assessment."

The supervisor turned his attention to the phone. "We have a breach. Centaur network." He nodded, then looked up at the screen. "It's the Software Validation site. Cincinnati."

The supervisor's face hardened as he listened to his orders. "Yes sir. Right away." He placed the phone back into the box, then put his arms rigidly behind his back He looked up at the Operations Center. "All hands on deck. Hide the code. Need a damage report in ten."

Another warning horn blared. All the operators stopped and looked up at the map. The thin red lines on the map begin spinning, slowly at first, then faster and faster. They dissolved into a pink blur that undulated briefly before congealing into the image of a Centaur, half-man, half-horse.

"Shit. We've got a runaway," the Midwest operator said.

The supervisor's face went blank. "Tell me one of you assholes did that."

The operators looked at each other momentarily, then dove back to their computers with a flurry of keystrokes.

Buck Winston put his cell phone, banded with a red stripe, back into his desk drawer and locked it. He slowly stood and stepped to the floor-to-ceiling glass wall and looked down over the sunlit Chicago skyline. After a moment, he went back to his desk and hit a button on his old-school desk phone.

"Yes, Mr. Winston?" came a reply over the speaker.

"Gwen, Senator Black's in town. Tell him I want him here at three."

"Right away, Mr. Winston."

Buck hit the button to kill the intercom, then took out his personal cell phone and hit a number.

Buck briefly waited, then: "What've you got close to Cincinnati?"

He stepped over to the window as he listened to the answer. "Okay. The software validation site. Send both teams. Also, I'm meeting Black at three. I want you here, too."

Gabby's phone buzzed. A text from Darek: "You have the riff now. Hope you like it."

Gabby disconnected the phone, put the cable into her backpack, the phone back into her pocket, and resumed her work.

After several hours of checking the computer output, Gabby's eyes were getting tired and the lines of code started to run together. She almost didn't spot it. "Hey Samar. You ever notice this?"

Samar came over to stand behind Gabby. He leaned down to get a look at a line of code Gabby was pointing at.

"Looks like a switch of some sort," Gabby said. "I haven't seen anything like it before."

"I remember seeing something like that the other day," Samar said. He stepped back over to his computer and sat down, typed a few strokes, then scrolled through the code. "Not there now. Kick it and see if it persists."

Gabby re-started the code sequence, then scrolled down through it. "That's weird." She intently stared at the line of code, tracing it with her finger. "It's gone. That shouldn't happen."

"Better make a note," Samar said.

Gabby nodded. She typed into her "Issue Log".

Buck Winston sat behind his desk. He lit a cigar, puffed on it to get it going. He offered the cigar box to Andre, who sat in one of the two chairs facing Buck's desk.

Andre shook his head, declining the offer.

They both looked up when Gwen knocked on Buck's half-open door.

Gwen stepped in with U. S. Senator Black, mid-60s, right behind her.

"The senator is here, sir. "Gwen said.

Senator Black quickly stepped around her. "What the fuck makes you think you can tell me when and where to be?"

Buck lifted his finger, silencing the senator. "Thanks Gwen."

Gwen nodded and stepped back out of the room, closing the door behind her.

Buck stayed in his seat. "Glad you could make it, Black."

Black stepped up to Buck's desk, his face red with anger. "That's Senator Black to you!"

Buck blew a ring of smoke.

Andre uncrossed his legs and straightened in his chair.

Black pointed at Andre: "Who the fuck's this?"

Winston smiled. "Settle down, Black. Have a seat."

Buck waved his cigar at Andre. "This is... well, you don't really need to know his name. All you need to know is he's getting ready to fix your most glorious fuck-up yet."

"What the hell are you talking about?"

"The voting certification bullshit."

Black pulled out a handkerchief and wiped his brow. "After that last fiasco of an election, the people needed to be able to trust the process."

Winston leaned forward, elbows on his desk. "And your dumb ass thought a public test of the software would do that?" He shook his head. "We were fine. Now I've got to clean up your shit."

A pair of cars screeched to a halt in front of the two-story software validation building. Several men, all wearing suits, emerged from the cars. They pulled sidearms as they raced for the building. The cars quickly pulled away.

Inside the software validation room, Gabby yawned and pulled off her headset. "Need some coffee. You?"

Samar didn't even look up. "No. Thanks."

"Okay. Back in a bit." She grabbed her backpack and phone.

She wandered down to the break room. It was empty. Gabby pulled a K-cup from her backpack and dropped it into the coffee maker. She checked her phone while she waited for the warm brew. The rapid CLICK, CLICK, CLICK of someone, several someones, running down the hall interrupted her. She stepped back so she could see through the window in the door.

A man, wearing a suit, flashed by.

What the hell? Instinctively, she stepped back so she couldn't be seen from the window. Another man raced by, holding a pistol.

The footsteps faded, so she slowly stepped toward the door, pulled it open a crack and looked down the hallway.

Nothing.

She retreated and grabbed her backpack, slung it onto her shoulder and quietly eased into the hallway. She carefully moved down the hall, stopping near the corner.

Cautiously, she stole a look around the corner toward the software testing room. Several men, all wearing similar suits, all carrying sidearms, stood near the door. One guy kicked in the door and another tossed something inside.

BOOM.

She jerked back, squatted down, holding her ears. *Samar?*

She took another look around the corner. Down the hallway, smoke poured from the testing room door. Two of the men drug Samar out of the room.

Gabby quickly looked around her. She spotted a fire alarm on the wall so she reached up and yanked it.

The fire alarm lights throughout the building instantly flashed off and on, accompanied by a loud, strobing audio tone that reverberated within the hallway.

She heard one of the men down the hall men yell above the noise of the alarm: "It's got to be the other one! Go!"

Gabby stood and raced back to the stairwell. She pushed the door open, ran inside and flew down the stairs. She leaped the last few steps to the landing where the staircase turned back on itself. She flew down the last steps to the first-floor door.

Above her, two men exploded through the door into the stairwell. A loud CRACK reverberated through the closed space.

Gabby heard a bullet ricochet off the concrete as she burst out into the hallway. She sprinted toward the lobby.

At the check-in booth, she spotted the guard, Henry, slumped over in his chair. She raced over to him, checked his pulse. Unconscious, but a big lump on the back of his head. She grabbed the revolver from his holster, flipped it over in her hand, spotted the safety and flipped it off just as the stairwell door behind her burst open.

She pushed Henry's chair with her foot, rolling Henry into a safer spot behind a concrete pillar. She pivoted toward her attackers, slightly squatted and brought the pistol up. BOOM. BOOM. Her gunshots echoed throughout the building entrance.

One of her attackers jerked back, grabbing his arm, the other raised his pistol and fired back. BOOM.

Gabby ducked down behind the reception desk. The bullet whizzed over her, driving a hole into the south window. She popped back up and fired off a quick round, then dropped back down as the stairwell door slammed shut. She glanced out the front window. In the fading daylight an ambulance pulled to a stop in front of the building, siren wailing.

Staying low, she moved to the security desk. She watched in the monitor as her two pursuers joined several other men in suits near the rear of the building. They drug Samar out through a emergency exit. Another monitor, pointed outside, showed a pair of cars pull up along the side street. The Suits rushed out and quickly loaded Samar into one of the cars. The rest of the men climbed into the other car and they raced away.

Gabby went to check on Henry as two medics entered through the front door. She glanced at them and saw a fire engine pulled in behind the ambulance.

Gabby slipped the revolver into her backpack, then stood and waved the medics over. She had to yell over the still blaring alarm: "Over here."

The medics hurried over. "What's going on?" one asked while the other checked out Henry.

"I was in the break room when the fire alarm went off. I came down to evacuate and found Henry like this."

Henry opened his eyes, jumped back in fear.

"Easy buddy. We got you," the medic told him.

Through the front window, Gabby saw a police car pull up near the fire truck. She patted Henry on the back and headed for the building entrance. She had to step aside as firefighters rushed to the front door and poured into the building.

Once the firefighters were in, Gabby stepped outside, her ever present backpack slung over her shoulder. She headed for the police vehicle, when her phone vibrated. Another text from Darek: *Don't talk to the cops.*

Gabby paused. She looked up at the police, just now getting out of their car, then back at her phone. She shook her head, but made a turn and joined a small group of on-lookers standing on the grass near the building.

Once the police moved into the building, she broke from the crowd and headed down the street, occasionally glancing back at the flurry of activity. She tapped her phone to call for an Uber, then nervously waited for it to arrive.

After the short ride, Gabby climbed out of the Uber and headed down the street. Once the Uber turned the corner, she cut back in the other direction, went into a dimly lit alley, then into a side door - a neon sign 'CLANCY'S' flashed above it.

There were only a few people inside the small lounge. A couple of patrons at the bar, and a several others at scattered tables.

The bartender, pouring a draft beer, nodded at Gabby. "Hey Gabs, you're allowed to use the front door again. Just so you know."

Gabby smiled and waved at the bartender. She made a bee line for a high-top table with three other people already seated, waiting for her to join in at their monthly reunion. She pulled out the only empty chair and climbed into it. "Hey guys."

"Gabby, you look like you've seen a ghost." Joel Baxter was a bit older than her, early thirties. He had been quite successful since they had gotten back from the sandbox, but Gabby knew he was miserably stuck in the corporate world. Tonight, his suit coat was draped over the back of his chair, a martini in front of him.

Gabby tried to smile. She looked over at Trish Irving. Trish was even a bit older, in her mid-thirties. Her United States Marine Corps tattoo graced her forearm from beneath her short-sleeved khaki shirt. A dark beer sat in front of her.

The last person at the table, Warren Maxwell, was even younger than Gabby, in his mid-twenties. Drexel Consulting was stenciled over the left breast of his pullover shirt. He sipped a White Russian.

Gabby pulled a round coin from her pocket and slapped it down in the middle, where it joined three other coins already there. The coins bore an image of Afghanistan, with the words "Joint Intelligence Operations Center" etched around the edge.

"Hell, Gabby," Warren said. "We didn't think you were coming."

"Thought you had to work tonight?" Trish said.

"Yeah, well. That's a whole story."

Joel winked at her. "Well, I can't wait to hear it."

"I need a drink first."

Joel yelled at the bartender: "Appletini for my girl, at your earliest convenience.

Gabby shook her head. "Not your girl." She looked back at the bartender and corrected Joel's order. "You know what I drink, Brad."

The bartender grinned and pulled a bottle down from the wall behind him. "I know it sure as hell ain't a 'appletini'. Bourbon. Straight."

Gabby gave him a thumbs up, then turned back to her group. "Any word from Darek?"

"You mean Merlin?" Trish asked.

"You know he hates being called that," Gabby said.

"Yeah, well. He needs to embrace it. He hasn't joined us for what, six months now?"

"I think he's still a little self-conscious about his leg," Warren took a sip from his drink.

"You can't even tell," Gabby said.

"I still can't figure out how he's the only one who got hit over there," Trish said. We all went outside the wire -- a lot more often than he did."

"Maybe someday he'll tell us what happened, Gabby said.

"I don't think he even lives there anymore," Joel said.

Gabby quickly looked at Joel. "Why's that?"

Joel leaned forward a bit. "I did a little checking around. No one at his old address. No forwarding info."

"If Darek doesn't want to be found, he won't be found," Warren said.

"Ain't that the truth," Trish agreed.

The bartender brought Gabby's drink. Everyone stopped talking until he left.

Gabby took a sip. "I got a couple of texts from him today."

Everyone at the table paused. They all stared at her.

Gabby looked down at her glass of bourbon, twisted the glass in her hand, then looked back up. "Guess I better tell you guys what happened."

"You are shittin' me," Joel said after Gabby finished telling them about her day. "Didn't Merlin get you that job?"

"He did?" Trish asked.

"Yeah. About two months ago. I got a cold call from a headhunter, asking if I wanted a part time gig while I was in school. Found out later Darek hooked me up."

"And now he's telling you not to talk to the police after you almost got killed?" Joel asked. "That son of a bitch set you up."

"He was always into some deep shit," Warren said. "Stuff he wouldn't tell us about."

"Couldn't tell us about," Gabby said. "That agency clown back at the Center had his hooks into Darek. Deep."

Joel finished his martini. "I think you should go to the cops. Let them know what's going on."

Trish shook her head. "Not a good idea. Not until we know who the suits are... who they work for."

Gabby's phone rang. She took it out of her pocket and checked the screen. "Darek."

Everyone looked at her.

"You gonna' answer?" Warren asked.

Gabby glanced at each of her friends, then put her phone in the middle of the table and hit the speaker icon. "Hi Darek. Got you on speaker. Everyone's here."

"Miss you, Merlin," Trish said.

They waited several moments before Darek spoke up. "Gabs, sorry for the SNAFU at your office. I didn't expect them to come that hard, or that fast."

Joel practically stood up, leaned forward to yell at the phone: "So you did set her up, you little prick!"

"Who's that?"

"It's Joel," Gabby said. "He's a little upset."

"Understandable," Darek replied. "Like I said, I didn't expect that response."

Gabby asked what she knew was on everyone's mind, including hers. "What's going on, Darek?"

"I'm sniffing out something. Something big. I'm pretty sure there's a fix in with the voting machines."

"We all know that," Warren said. "Domain Corporation. Their voting software's rigged."

"That's just a conspiracy theory," Joel said through clenched teeth.

"Maybe, maybe not," Darek said. "I think it's something darker. Goes to the heart of our entire political framework. That's why I didn't want you going to the cops, Gabs."

"This is fuckin' nuts!" Joel said.

"Gabs, that switch you saw in the code wasn't a fluke," Darek said. "I downloaded some of the program, but I need some help analyzing it. Warren, you up?"

"Damn straight!' Warren said.

"How'd you know about the switch?" Gabby asked.

"I'll have to explain that part later, Gabs. Warren, I uploaded what I've de-compiled to Gabby's cloud back-up. Let me know what you find."

The phone unexpectedly went dead.

Everyone looked at each other in brief silence.

"I think we all need another round." Joel waved at the bartender, then turned back to the table. "How the hell did he get the code from the voting machine?"

"Good question," Trish said.

"Oh. Yeah, I didn't mention that part," Gabby said. "I plugged my phone into the computer I was working on. Darek wanted to send me a new riff."

"Brilliant," Joel shook his head. "Whoever's network you plugged into, their intrusion detection system probably has your name, rank, phone number, serial number, address, every fuckin' thing. Merlin set you up good."

"He wouldn't do that," Gabby said. "Not on purpose."

In a dark warehouse, a man in a suit placed an empty syringe into a leather pouch. He held his phone to his ear.

Behind him, under a bright light, Samar sat unconscious, tied to a chair.

"Go." Andre said on the other end of the line.

The man in the suit made his report: "He doesn't know anything, but he rambled some stuff about a girl."

"What girl?" Andre asked.

"Probably the one who shot at us."

Andre lit a cigarette in his darkened room living room. He spoke into his phone. "Track her down. Use him as bait if you have to."

Andre cancelled the call, then dialed another number.

It rang. Buck Winston picked up the call on the other end. "Tell me it's taken care of."

Andre took a drag on his cigarette: "Not yet. I'd better head over there."

There was a brief pause, then Winston replied: "Okay. The jet will be waiting. I want this zipped up. Now!"

Gabby downed the last of her bourbon.

"Can I see your phone?" Warren asked.

Gabby pushed her thumb against the phone to unlock it, then slid it across the table.

Trish laid out possible courses of action while Warren examined Gabbie's phone. "Okay, so the options are:" Trish flipped up her index finger, "Go to the cops." She flipped up another finger." Don't go to the cops, and hope it goes away, or," finger three, "Go on the offense."

Gabby shook her head: "Going to the cops isn't an option." She thought briefly. "And I'm not going to sit back and wait for those assholes to come to me, but we don't have enough info to go on the offense."

Warren showed Trish what he found on Gabby's phone. "The file's here, like Darek said. Whatever he downloaded, auto-backup put a copy in the cloud. I pushed it over to my server. I'll have to go home to take a good look."

"I need to check on Samar," Gabby pushed her chair back and stood up. "I'm sure his wife is going nuts. At least I can tell her what I saw."

"You aren't going by yourself," Joel stood and grabbed his suit coat. "'They might still be after you. I'll be your backup."

Gabby nodded.

"'You want some help with the file?" Trish asked Warren.

"I'll take all the help I can get."

They left separately, Trish went with Warren and Joel with Gabby.

Joel drove while Gabby leaned back in the seat, eyes closed.

"Did you notice Trish and Warren?" Joel asked. "Seems like they may have a little something going on."

Gabby looked over at him, then rolled her eyes. "They hooked up before we came home. Been together ever since." She looked over at Joel. "You really are clueless sometimes."

Joel shrugged. "Maybe, about some things. He briefly looked over at Gabby, then back to the road. "I still don't understand why you trust Darek."

"You don't know him like I do. He pulled my ass out of the fire more than once."

"Somehow I think it was probably the other way around. He was just a frickin' keyboard warrior."

Gabby shook her head. "No, you're wrong. You didn't get there 'til the end. Before you got there, the spooks used him a lot. In and out of the field.

"You, too?"

Gabby smiled and looked over at him. "I'd tell you..."

Joel looked back at her, smiling as well.

"But then I'd have to kill you," they said in unison.

Joel looked back at the road, eyes straight ahead. After a moment, he asked: "You guys had a thing, didn't you?"

Gabby ignored him.

The car's GPS flashed. Joel pulled to the side of the street. "This is it."

It wasn't far to the apartment building. They went inside and easily found the right apartment. Gabby and Joel stood in the hallway outside the door. Gabby hesitated, looked over at Joel.

He nodded.

Gabby knocked.

The door opened and a mid-eastern woman looked out through red, swollen eyes. She burst into tears and reached forward to hug Gabby. "Oh... Gabby... What is happening?"

Gabby wrapped her arms around the woman. "It's going to be okay, Nasira."

Gabby spotted Samar inside the apartment. He sat in a well-worn chair, a frost covered bag of peas pressed against the side of his head. Gabby let go of Nasira and rushed inside: "Samar!"

Nasira grabbed Joel's sleeve and pulled him inside.

Gabby knelt down beside Samar and took his hand.

Samar's eyes were unfocused, he barely turned to look at Gabby.

"Samar? Are you alright?"

Samar didn't answer.

Nasira knelt down beside Gabby and took Samar's other hand. "I don't know what's wrong. He only came home fifteen minutes ago, and he was like this." Nasira burst into tears.

Gabby wrapped her arm around Nasira's shoulders. "It's okay... It's okay.

After a moment, Nasira's sobbing quieted.

"Has he said anything?" Gabby asked.

Nasira shook her head. "Only that his head was in pain. What should I do?"

"We should call 9-1-1," Joel said.

Gabby shot Joel a cold look. She turned back and looked into Samar's eyes. "Samar? Can you hear me?"

Samar turned his head slightly toward Gabby.

Gabby reached forward and pushed up one of Samar's eyelids. She studied first one eye, then the other. She breathed a sigh of relief. "You're going to be okay, Samar."

Gabby turned to Nasira. "Give him half an hour and he should snap out of it. Call me if he says anything, okay?"

Nasira nodded, never taking her eyes off of Samar. She stroked her husband's arm as she held his hand.

Joe Gribble

Gabby nodded at Joel and they headed out of the apartment and back down to Joel's car.

Joel slipped the car in drive and pulled out. "Why not call 9-1-1?"

Gabby squirmed in her seat. "Their visas are expired. Hospitals ask too many questions."

Neither of them noticed a car parked down the street. It pulled out, lights off, and followed from a distance.

"You really think he'll be okay?" Joel asked.

"Yeah, he's just been scoped."

"Scoped?"

"The way he acted. His eyes. Scopolamine. Truth serum. It's an Agency favorite."

"The fuckin' Agency's behind this?"

Warren's name popped up on the car display, accompanied by a jingle. Joel pushed a button on his steering wheel to answer the call.

"Find anything?" Gabby asked.

"*Yeah. Tons,*" Warren said over the phone. "*The switch you found. It's a mechanical call-out.*"

"Mechanical? To what?

"*Input output to the power supply. These machines are supposed to be stand-alone - disconnected from the net. That's what doesn't make sense. The code, it's connecting to something via the power grid.*"

"How is that even possible?" Joel asked.

"*Power company does it all the time,*" Trish said over the phone. "*That's how they read your meter.*"

"Yeah, but those are dedicated power line comm circuits. Very limited capability. They can't communicate through transformers. Only over the air," Warren said.

Gabby shook her head. "The switch I saw in the code disappeared. Even I know what that means."

"*Yeah,*" Warren said. "*Someone commanded the machine to hide the code. And you can't command if you can't communicate.*"

"Then we're back to the big question," Joel said. "How?"

"And who?" Gabby asked.

In Warren's basement, Warren sat in front of an array of five monitors - one big one in the center and four smaller ones, two on each side of the main screen. A computer game played on one of the small monitors. Code trickled up and down on the others.

Trish sat beside Warren.

Warren's phone sat on the table. He spoke into an attached mike/speaker. "I don't know the answer to either of those, but the code's definitely connecting to the power circuit." He grabbed a joystick and engaged a creature in the game.

"*You figured that out pretty fast,*" Gabby said.

Trish rolled back in her chair and Warren moved over to get a better look at the game. "He'll try and take credit for it, but Merlin posted up the de-compiled code. I'm betting he laid some pretty obvious crumbs."

Warren threw his hands up as his game character blew up in a fireball. "That's all the code can tell us, though. We have to get our hands on one of the machines if we want to find out how it's connecting to the power circuits. How it's communicating."

Back in Joel's car, the two pondered their dilemma. Joel turned left. "Just how the hell are we supposed to do that?" He didn't notice the car behind him, lights still out, illuminated only briefly by a street lamp. The car turned to follow them.

"*There's gotta' be a machine we can get a look at,*" Warren said over the phone.

Gabby's phone chimed. Another text from Darek, with an address: 4215 Grissom St, Mason OH. "Darek just texted me an address."

"*I got it, too,*" Warren said.

Joel squeezed the steering wheel. "Fuckin' Merlin is listening to our call? How the hell's he doing that?"

In Warren's lair, Warren switched to a map application and keyed in the address. He expanded the image, focusing on the pointer location. "It's a warehouse."

Trish stopped tapping away at a laptop keyboard and looked up. "Ohio Secretary of State's office holds the lease."

Joel and Gabby heard Trish's comment in the car. Joel made another left turn.

Gabby looked over at him. "I'm guessing that's where we can find a voting machine."

"You seriously trust Merlin?" Joel asked. "I doubt anyone at that warehouse is going to just hand us a voting machine."

"Then, we'll have to borrow it."

"Are you nuts?"

"Look, those assholes tried to kill me. I need to figure this out."

"Like I said, we go to the cops."

Gabby's phone dinged again. Another text from Darek. Gabby read it and looked up. "Darek says not to go to the cops."

Joel squeezed the steering wheel tightly. "That guy is getting on my nerves."

Gabby leaned her head back, eyes closed for a few seconds. She quickly sat back up, eyes open. "Guys, I need to get one of those machines. This is probably illegal, so I can't ask you to help." She paused and looked over at Joel. "But I really need your help."

Warren chimed in over the phone. *"Oh, hell yeah. I've been bored out of my fuckin' mind the last six months."*

Trish joined in: *"Just like the good ol' days. We're a team again."*

Joel looked straight ahead. Silent.

Gabby spoke to the others. "Okay. Thanks, you guys. I'm going to my place to grab some gear. Meet you at the warehouse at..." she glanced at the clock on the dashboard: 12:15. "Let's say 'oh one thirty'. That work?"

Warren and Trish answered in unison: *"We'll be there."*

Gabby reached up to push a button on the car console, killing the call. She looked over at Joel. "I can't ask you to help. You're actually doing well, and this could really screw up your corporate gig."

Joel still stared straight ahead. "I'll take you to your apartment." They drove in silence for a few minutes, before he continued. "I really can't take the chance. If we get busted, my whole world would come crashing down."

Gabby reached up and put her hand on his, still tightly clenching the steering wheel. "I understand. I really do."

Joel's hands relaxed. He looked over at Gabby with a smile. "Besides, someone will have to bail your asses out of jail."

It wasn't long before Joel pulled to a stop outside a long row of two-story apartment buildings.

Half a block behind, the car following them, lights still out, pulled to the curb. A man in a suit got out of the passenger's seat.

Gabby released her seat belt, reached into the back for her backpack, then pulled on the door handle. She paused, looked back at Joel: "I know you don't trust Darek, but you should."

"It's not that I don't trust him. I've just never been really sure where his loyalties are."

Gabby shook her head. "Thanks for the ride."

"Anything for my girl."

"Again, not your girl." She climbed out and walked toward the apartment entrance. She opened the door, then turned and waved back at Joel.

Joel watched from inside his car until Gabby went inside the building, then pulled away.

A shadow crossed some bushes near the apartment building door.

Gabby went inside the vestibule to that section of apartments. It was small, and well represented the rest of the building. Not dingy, but far from elegant. Only one of the fluorescent light bulbs gave off any light, making it somewhat dark. Two apartment doors bracketed a small staircase that led up to the second floor.

Gabby bounded up the steps, two at a time, then turned to the apartment on the right. She pulled a set of keys from her backpack and unlocked the door.

The man in the suit waited outside. Watching. A light came on in one of the second story apartments. He keyed a small microphone on his lapel. "Got her."

"On my way," came the reply.

He crept along the side of the building, assessing the apartment layout.

Down the street, the driver, also wearing a suit (Suit Two) killed the engine and quietly opened his car door. He stepped out, and gently pushed the door closed. He checked the pistol in his shoulder holster, then quickly walked toward Gabby's apartment.

Inside the apartment, Gabby tossed her backpack on the sofa and headed for the adjoining kitchen. She opened the fridge and peered inside. A half-full jug of chocolate milk caught her eye. She pulled it out and chugged some down.

Now almost two blocks away, Joel stopped at a light. His phone rang again through the radio speaker. Gabby's number. "Hey Gabs."

But it wasn't Gabby on the phone. "It's Darek."

"How'd you get Gabby's phone."

"I didn't. I knew you wouldn't pick up if you knew it was me."

"You sure as hell got that right."

"Gabby's in trouble."

"No shit? All your doing, too."

"No, you idiot. She's in trouble NOW - at her apartment. I'm too far away. She needs your help. Hurry."

Joel cut his wheel sharply and burned a U-turn at the red light. He stomped the accelerator and raced back toward Gabby's apartment. "If anything happens to her.." The line went dead.

Outside Gabby's apartment, Suit 1 and Suit 2 met up at the corner, in the shadow of the building. Using hand signals, Suit 1 pointed at the upper apartment with the light on. He pointed at his chest, then at a small balcony with a sliding glass door on the second floor.

Suit 2 nodded. He pointed at the front door.

Suit 1 moved to a small trellis adjacent to the balcony.

Suit 2 waited until Suit 1 was half way up the trellis, then pulled his pistol and made his way in the shadows to the front door. He checked for observers, then slipped inside.

Suit 1 quietly climbed over the rail onto the balcony. He hid in the shadows against the wall and waited.

Inside the apartment, Gabby's phone buzzed. A text from Darek: "Check your six. And your twelve."

She glanced over at her apartment door just as it exploded inward.

She grabbed a small kitchen knife off the counter and rushed toward the assault.

Behind her, the glass in her balcony door shattered inward with a loud crash.

Suit 2 came through the front door, leading with his pistol.

Gabby attacked low and from the side. She spotted the Suit's weapon as he ran in. She sliced upward with the knife, cutting his forearm,

Suit 2 yelled out in pain, dropping his gun. He dodged Gabby's next parry, then with his good arm he grabbed Gabby by her wrist and pulled her in front of him, twisted her around and wrapped her in a bear hug.

Gabby slammed her head backward, crushing Suit 2's nose.

Dazed, Suit 2 loosened his grip.

Gabby fought her way out of the bear hug and twisted the Suit's bleeding arm back up and around his back.

Suit 2 howled in agony.

Gabby continued twisting his arm, but saw a hand reach through the broken glass of the balcony door and twist the lock open

Gabby glanced over at the pistol on the floor. She released Suit 2's arm and dove toward the weapon. She got to it, rolled over behind the sofa and popped up to fire off a round at the new intruder.

BOOM.

She missed. Suit 1 was already inside. He leaped behind the kitchen wall and peered around the corner.

Suit 2 regained his composure and jumped toward Gabby. He grabbed her leg and yanked it out from under her, then stood to drag her backwards.

Face first on the floor, Gabby was yanked violently backwards. She rolled over, face up, and pulled the pistol up to fire.

Suit 1 had raced from his hidden position and lunged down on her, fighting her for the pistol.

BOOM. Gabby pulled the trigger again. She barely missed Suit 1's ear.

He twisted Gabby's wrist hard and the pistol fell to the floor. The Suits had her by two arms and a leg and began dragging her toward the door.

Gabby kicked her free leg at Suit 2, but to no avail.

Suit 2 tried to grab Gabby's free leg, but she kicked at him again. He gave up and continued to drag her, backing toward the apartment door.

Joel burst in. He grabbed Suit 1 from behind and tried to break his grip on Gabby's arms.

Suit 1 wouldn't let go.

Gabby flailed. She pulled Suit 1's arm close to her mouth and bit down hard on his thumb.

Suit 1's grip loosened and Joel ripped his arms loose from Gabby, then lifted the man up bodily and slammed him down on Gabby's rickety coffee table. The table splintered and Suit 1 crashed all the way to the floor.

Suit 2 continued pulling on Gabby's leg, bent over, trying to drag her to the door.

With her arms now free, she grabbed a broken coffee table leg, jagged on one end. She curled up and crowned Suit 2, sending him staggering backwards.

Joel jumped on top of Suit 1, still prone on top of the remnants of the coffee table, and started pummeling him.

Suit 1 used his arms to protect himself and used his legs to flip Joel off of him sideways. They grappled on the floor. Suit 1 managed to get behind Joel. He grabbed Joel's tie and pulled it tight around his neck.

A siren wailed in the background.

Suit 1 looked up. Suit 2 slowly climbed back to his feet, still staggering from the blow he received from Gabby.

Gabby rolled over. Suit 1 held Joel's tie tight around his neck.

Joel fought back, but he struggled for air, his face already a dark red.

Gabby lunged forward and jabbed the pointed end of the coffee table leg into Suit 1's thigh.

Suit 1 screamed in agony, releasing his grip on Joel's tie.

Joel coughed, almost unconscious from the choke hold.

Suit 1 pulled the wooden stake from his leg, releasing a torrent of blood. He struggled to a standing position, then hobbled over to grab Suit 2. Suit 2 half carried, half dragged Suit 1 to the door.

Gabby scrambled over to where the pistol lay forgotten on the floor. She grabbed it and turned, but the Suits were already out the door. She cautiously stepped over to the apartment door, then took a quick look out into the stairwell. No one. She started down after them.

The sirens grew louder. Closer.

Joel yelled from up in the apartment. "Gabby!"

Blue and red lights flashed through the stairwell window and reflected off the walls inside. Gabby quickly retreated back up to the apartment.

Joel worked to release the knot in his tie and pull it from around his neck. "Always hated these damned things."

Gabby raced past him into her bedroom.

Joel followed, tossing his tie to the floor.

She opened her closet door and yanked out a wooden box, tossing it on the bed.

"This would be a good time to come clean with the cops," Joel suggested.

She looked up at him, quickly opening the box. "Seriously? And say what. Some people I don't know are trying to kill me?"

Gabby pulled out a tactical vest and two pistols. She pulled the vest on and loaded a pistol into a holster on each side. Four other loaded magazines went into vest pockets.

"You're going full auto, then?" Joel asked.

"I don't think I have a choice." She pulled a knife out of the box, strapped it to her ankle, then grabbed the two remaining mags and rushed back to the living room.

She stuffed the extra mags into her backpack and grabbed her phone. She headed toward the front door, but paused when she heard the vestibule door open below.

Joel stepped out of the bedroom door as Gabby rushed over to the shattered balcony door. "Unless you want to talk to the cops..."

She stepped toward the balcony, but Joel stopped her.

He turned off the light and quickly glanced out onto the balcony. "Clear," he said quietly, then waved for Gabby to follow him out.

Joel climbed over the rail and onto the trellis. "Come on," he said, still quietly.

Gabby shook her head. She put her hands on the balcony rail and leaped over, dropping all the way to the ground. She landed, cat-like, in a crouch.

Joel dropped the last few feet to the ground. "Seriously? You could have broken your leg."

The flashing lights out front grew in number.

"We can't go to your car," Gabby said. "Follow me."

Gabby headed away from the street at a jog. Joel followed behind, constantly glancing back.

Gabby stopped at a long, one-story shed and moved around to the far side. She went to the third garage door, opened the keypad cover and punched in her code.

The door opened and the light inside came on. Cardboard boxes took up most of the garage, but in the middle sat a grape-colored Suzuki 'crotch rocket', poised to race out the door.

Joel caught up with her and looked inside. "Oh, hell no. You aren't getting me on that."

Gabby tossed him a helmet. "No choice."

She peeled off her backpack and handed it to him as well. "Put this on and climb on behind me. Just lean into the curves."

Gabby mounted the bike without a helmet. She pushed a button and the machine grumbled to life.

Joel struggled to pull on the tight helmet, then slung the backpack onto his back. "You don't go anywhere without this thing, do you?"

"Some girls carry purses." Gabby stood the machine up and heeled the kickstand back. "Come on, already."

Joel tentatively climbed on behind her.

Gabby eased the clutch out and slowly, as quietly as possible, pulled out of the garage.

Joel wrapped his arms around her waist.

"Watch your hands!" Gabby told him. She crept down the access road.

"This isn't so bad," Joel said.

At the end of the access road, Gabby turned opposite the rapidly congealing mass of police cars. She maintained a slow speed for half a block, then slowly accelerated. "Hang on." She gunned the throttle as they passed the next road. The two-wheeled missile launched forward.

Joel almost fell off the bike backwards. "Ohhhh Shitttt....". He grabbed tighter around her waist and pulled himself back onto the seat.

"I told you to hang on." She took two curves at high speed.

Joel leaned away from the turn, trying to stay upright.

Gabby yelled back at him over the wind: "Just lean with me. Don't fight it." She took the next curve even faster. "Better. Where do you want me to drop you?"

Joel yelled back: "Swing by my condo. I'll get my gear."

"What for?"

"I'm going with you. No one messes with my girl."

Gabby smiled and turned her head to yell at him. "Not your girl."

It didn't take more than fifteen minutes to make it to Joel's condo. Gabby parked her bike in the driveway to the three-car garage and they went inside.

Gabby stood next to the burning gas fireplace, waiting in the living room of Joel's swanky condo.

Joel came out of the bedroom wearing a nearly all-black ensemble. Two pistols adorned his vest – similar to Gabby's. "Like Warren said: Just like the old days!"

Gabby flipped a wall switch, extinguishing the gas flame. She stepped toward the door. "You still know how to use those?"

Joel pulled one of the pistols, racked the slide back to chamber a round. "It's like riding a bike, you never forget." He tried to re-holster the pistol, but accidentally hit the magazine release and the mag clanged to the floor.

Gabby stopped and turned to look at Joel as he scrambled to grab the mag. "Looks like you still have the training wheels on your bike."

Joel slammed the mag back into the pistol, holstered it, then pulled a small jacket on over his vest. "Could happen to anyone. Speaking of bikes, let's leave yours here. We'll take my other ride."

They went out through the front door to the driveway where Gabby's motorcycle waited.

Joel hit a button on his keychain and the garage door opened.

Multiple bright lights lit the pristine space in the garage. Uncluttered, the space on the left was empty, while on the right sat a brand-new Hummer.

Gabby pushed her bike into the empty stall, then joined Joel in the Hummer.

Gabby's phone buzzed as she pulled her seat belt on. "Warren and Trish are already there."

Joel started the engine and shifted into gear. "Tell them to Recon. We're fifteen minutes out."

Andre angrily spoke into his phone from the back of the limo. "It's starting to sound like I hired the wrong men for this job. Get your asses to the warehouse, that's where they'll head next. Keep her alive until I get there."

He terminated the call and looked up at the driver. "Move it!"

Joel pulled up to the warehouse and parked next to a seventies style van. Mag wheels, dual exhaust, and Scooby-Doo paint scheme.

Gabby and Joel exited the Hummer and walked up to the van's sliding side door. Gabby grabbed the handle and yanked it open. A single street light across the road lit up the interior of the van through the windshield. They climbed into the two second-row captain's chairs behind Warren in the driver's seat and Trish riding shotgun.

"Look at you two, all dressed up for the party," Trish said.

"What'd you find?" Gabby asked.

Warren held up his phone so Gabby could see a video of their reconnaissance of the building. "Piece of cake."

"No security?" Joel asked.

"No guards," Warren answered. "But there's an Altim two thousand 'X'. State-of-the-art alarm system." He grinned. "State-of-the-art fifteen years ago."

"Dumb ass government," Trish said.

"Can you disarm it?" Gabby asked.

"I can give us about twenty minutes. After twenty with no signal, the system will alert the cops."

"Twenty minutes should be plenty," Trish said.

Warren handed each of them a small radio, with ear pieces.

"Where'd you get these?" Joel asked.

"Five finger discount before we left the sandbox."

Everyone put their radios into a pocket in the upper left front of their matching vests. Tailored fit. Ear pieces went into their ears.

The intrepid four quietly exited the van and made their way up to their target. They stole around the side of the building, staying in the shadows, then approached a short set of steps leading to a door, adjacent to a loading dock.

A motion sensor operated light flashed on above the door, well out of reach.

"Shit." Joel pulled his pistol and aimed it at the light.

Gabby grabbed his arm. "Don't. The noise will attract a lot more attention than the light." She waved to Warren.

Warren and Trish moved forward, toward the stairs.

Trish waited at the base of the stairs, keeping lookout, while Warren nonchalantly climbed the steps. After a quick glance around, Warren pulled a screwdriver from a large tool belt wrapped around his waist. He forcefully jammed it into the side of a circuit box near the door. The circuit box door popped open.

Warren turned on his forehead mounted light and stared at the wires inside. From his belt he pulled out a small wire with alligator clips on either end and attached the ends to screws inside the box. With a small pair of clippers, he cut a wire. He looked back and gave a thumbs up.

Gabby and Joel moved out of the shadows.

Warren stepped over to the main door lock, just below a large bar that served as the handle. He briefly studied it, then held his hand up.

Gabby and Joel paused, then stepped back into the cover.

Trish quickly looked around, then gave Warren a thumbs up.

Warren took a noise-dampened, battery-powered drill out of his tool belt and made quick work of the key lock. It popped out and he used the same screwdriver to pry out the dead bolt.

Warren turned and smiled, then gave another thumbs up.

Gabby and Joel again stepped out of the shadows and rushed, bent low, toward the door.

Once there, they found Warren and Trish both pulling on the handle. The door remained stubbornly closed.

Warren gave up pulling on it. "Shit. They must have it barred inside."

"Some great B and E man you are," Joel said.

"He couldn't have known," Trish said.

"Well, what next?" Joel asked.

"We'll have to go old school and yank it off. I have a chain in the van."

"I'll get the Hummer," Joel said.

Warren tried to stop him: "I don't..." But Joel was already walking away, fishing keys out of his pocket.

Warren turned back to Trish and Gabby. "Stay out of sight for a bit."

Warren headed to his van while Trish and Gabby retreated into the shadows.

Joel pulled up in his Hummer. He spun around, then started backing up to the door, an annoying, and none too quiet, BEEP.... BEEP.... BEEP emanated from the Hummer's backup warning system.

Warren ran up with a large chain.

Joel stopped the Hummer and climbed out, heading around to the back.

"Good God!" Warren said. "Can't you find a louder way to announce us?"

Warren quickly climbed the few steps to the door, wrapped the chain around the handle twice and locked it off. He pulled the other end of the chain down to the Hummer.

Joel grabbed the end of the chain and wrapped it around the ball hitch on his bumper.

"Are you sure this'll hold?" Warren asked.

Joel locked off the chain, leaving some slack, then patted the side of his Hummer. "Better step back."

Joel climbed back into the Hummer. He slowly pulled forward, drawing the slack out of the chain. The Hummer stopped when the chain grew taut. Joel pushed down on the accelerator.

All four tires slowly spun on the asphalt, turning faster and faster, eventually generating a wisp of blue smoke.

The door didn't budge.

Joel floored the truck, but the wheels just spun faster, billowing a huge cloud of blue smoke, tires screaming in protest.

He finally gave up and stopped.

Warren ran up to his window. "You're going to have to jerk it. But I don't know if your bumper..."

Joel ignored him and slipped the truck into reverse. He backed up a couple of feet, accompanied by the annoying BEEP...BEEP... Joel dropped it into drive and gave it the gas. The truck quickly moved forward, but slammed to a stop when the chain went taut. The door budged, but didn't give. "God damn it!"

He backed up again, even further, then dropped the Hummer in "LOW" and stomped on the gas. The Hummer lurched forward. The chain snapped tight and, accompanied by the sound of a small explosion, the Hummer jerked to a brief stop as the ball hitch, and attached bumper, ripped from the frame and loudly clattered to the ground. The Hummer, untethered, lurched forward again. Joel stood on the brakes and leaped out, forgetting to put it into park. He dove dive back into the rolling truck to stop it. He slammed it into park and rushed back out.

Warren stood there, looking at the mangled rear end of Joel's Hummer: "Your bumper fell off."

"No shit!" Joel said.

Trish called over the radio: "We're already ten minutes down."

Warren nodded. "Time to get to work. Move your truck. I'll get the van."

Moments later the Scooby van whipped into the lot, spun around and quietly backed up to the door.

The Hummer sat nearby, the back door open and the bumper lying inside.

Warren jumped out and ran to the back. He grabbed the end of the chain, dropped down on his back and wriggled under the van.

Joel squatted down to watch Warren: "You really think this van will hold up when the Hummer wouldn't?

Warren spoke from under the van: "Nineteen Seventy-Two. Three quarter ton frame." He climbed back out from under the van and rushed back into the driver's seat. "Yeah, it'll hold up." He grinned, dropped the van into drive and crushed the accelerator.

Joe Gribble

The van's rear tires briefly squealed as it lurched forward. The chain pulled taut yet again, but this time the building door exploded outward. The reinforced steel door bounced twice at the end of the chain before the van screeched to a stop.

Gabby and Trish rushed out of the shadows and disappeared inside the building.

Joel helped Warren disconnect the chain from the van and the door. They threw the chain inside the van and Warren backed up to the steps again.

Gabby and Trish met them at the back door with a large box riding on a furniture dolly.

The four of them ushered the dolly and box down the three steps, then leaned the box over and shoved it into the van.

Out at the road, a small, white car, 'SECURITY' emblazoned on the front door, pulled to a stop on a road about one hundred feet from the warehouse. A search light clicked on. The beam flashed onto the building, then crept toward the loading dock.

On that same road, from the other direction, a pair of sedans raced toward the warehouse.

Back at the warehouse, Gabby and Trish wrestled the box containing the voting machine into the van.

"Let's get another one, for backup," Trish said.

Gabby nodded and followed Trish back into the building, Joel hot on their heels.

Warren followed, but a set of headlights flashed behind him and he looked back toward the road. "We have company," he shouted, warning the others.

Joel glanced back, saw the bright light coming from the security car. "We gotta' go!" he yelled into the warehouse.

Warren slammed the van's rear door shut just as the spotlight from the security guard flashed on them. Warren ran up to the driver's door, jumped in and cranked the engine. The engine turned over and over, but didn't start. "Shit." He yelled out the window: "Let's go!"

Joel stepped inside the warehouse door and briefly waited for his eyes to adjust to the darkness. A pile of boxes near the door blocked his view. He stepped around them and saw a light a dozen feet away. Gabby and Trish were working another voting machine box, of the hundreds in the warehouse, onto a dolly. "Leave it!" he yelled.

The women abandoned their effort and ran toward Joel.

"What is it?" Gabby asked.

"Security. Come on."

"Shit." Trish pulled out her handgun and rushed out the door, Joel and Gabby right behind her.

Gabby tripped on a box in the dark, and she crashed to the floor.

Joel stopped and ran back to help her up. "You okay?"

Gabby noticed he held her a little closer than needed, his eyes staring into hers. A brief spark. She found herself holding him a little tight as well.

"Quit playing grab ass!" Trish yelled from the door. "Let's go!"

Gabby broke contact first, then turned and ran toward the door.

They raced past another stack of boxes. The boxes were smaller. A graphic of a TV antenna 'dish' adorned the outside of each box.

Back outside, Warren was still cranking the van's engine. No luck.

Off in the distance, the security guard yelled: "Stop what you're doing right now. Raise your hands!"

Trish leveled her pistol.

Gabby pushed Trish's arm down, stopping her from shooting. "He's just a working dude."

Warren cranked the van again. Still no joy.

"Leave the van," Joel said as he jumped into his Hummer.

"No way," Warren replied as he cranked it again. The starter now turned noticeably slower.

Gabby ran to Joel's Hummer and slung open the passenger door. She yelled back at Warren. "He's right, Warren. Leave it. Come on!"

In the distance, two cars slid to a stop near the guard.

A pair of men, both wearing suits, got out of one of the cars.

The guard, standing outside the driver's door of his security vehicle, turned a handle inside the car door, causing his floodlight to spin back at the approaching men.

The men both shaded their eyes from the bright light.

"Easy, brother," the man on the right said. "Homeland security."

The other man slowly reached for his inside pocket. "Getting my credentials." He brought out a wallet as the two men continued to step toward the cop. The man flipped his wallet open to expose his badge.

The guard cautiously reached for the wallet when the first man quickly stepped beside the guard and WHACKED him with a pistol butt.

The guard dropped.

One of the men waved to the other car.

The car's wheels threw gravel as it launched toward the warehouse.

Back at the warehouse, Joel pointed at one of the cars in the distance as its headlights flashed toward them, growing larger and larger. "Shit. Those aren't working dudes."

Gabby jumped back out of the Hummer. She pulled her gun as she moved up to the right front fender. She squatted slightly and braced her arms on top of the hood. Keeping her eyes on the inbound threat, she yelled at Warren: "Come on, Warren. We gotta' move."

Warren looked over at Gabby, then looked to where her gun pointed. The oncoming lights were barreling toward them. "Shit." He twisted the key again. Still no life from the engine.

BOOM. Gabby's hands bucked up and back as the round left her gun. One of the headlights in the oncoming car shattered and went dark.

Trish ran over to the Scooby van and ducked down behind the front passenger fender. She leveled her gun and fired next. A trail of sparks bounced along the side of the oncoming car.

The car didn't slow. Two flashes from its windows warned of return fire.

Inside the Scooby van, a crack in the passenger side of the windshield spidered across to the driver's side, a round bullet hole in the passenger's side marked the source of the damage.

Warren ducked. He pumped the accelerator several times, then twisted the key in one last attempt.

Trish fired again, then yelled: "Come on, Warren."

A round smacked into the Hummer's bumper. Gabby squeezed off another shot, then looked back at the Scooby van. A low BOOM belched from the Scooby exhaust pipe, followed by a cloud of white smoke, and sounds of the engine struggling to life.

Warren lovingly patted the steering wheel. "Yeah, baby!"

Trish jumped into the passenger's side of the van, just as Warren dropped it into gear, launching toward the lights bearing down on them.

Trish rolled down her window and continued to shoot.

Behind them, the Hummer lurched forward, somewhat slower than Warren's, and fell in line behind the Scooby van.

A game of chicken quickly played out. The oncoming car rapidly gained speed, racing straight at the Scooby van.

The Scooby van waddled, but also gained momentum.

Warren drove crouched down, barely able to see over the dashboard.

Trish stayed low, too. She put her pistol through her open window. "Assholes." She ripped off three quick rounds. Sparks flew from the oncoming car's hood, then the windshield.

The oncoming car swerved sideways onto the grass, spinning in a half circle.

Right behind the Scooby van, Joel floored his Hummer, trying to keep up with Warren and Trish.

Gabby pulled on her seat belt. They both watched the oncoming car as it spun into the grass, slowed, then started moving forward to follow them.

Ahead in the Scooby van, Warren and Trish passed the damaged car. "They're still coming," Trish said. Ahead, flashes from near the security car resulted in yet another hole in the Scooby van's windshield.

"Shit," Warren said as he yanked the steering wheel to the left. The van bounced off the edge of the asphalt and into the grass. He pressed forward as more bullets PING'ed off the passenger side of the van. Trish continued to return fire at the assailants.

Back in the Hummer, Joel was still trying to catch up when he saw the van head into the grass. "Where the hell's he going?" Flashes from near the security car and a loud PING from up front clued him in.

"Follow Warren!" Gabby yelled as she ducked down. She pressed the button to roll down her window, then returned fire.

Inside the Scooby van, Warren punched the accelerator.

Trish glanced through the cracked windshield. They were hurtling toward a line of large bushes. "Watch out!" she yelled.

"Hang on!" Warren loudly replied. He tightly gripped the steering wheel as Trish braced herself against the dashboard. The Scooby van crashed through the bushes, then down into a small ditch. The van bucked up and out of the ditch, violently tossing its occupants around. The van slowed, then slammed to a stop as it hit top dead center on a berm below them.

Trish and Warren both jerked forward, held back only by their seat belts. "OOF!" they dumped their breaths in unison.

Joel and Gabby watched as the Scooby van hurtled through the bushes and disappeared. They saw the van's tail lights viciously bounce up and down, then come to a stop.

Joel eased up on the gas pedal and they slowed. "He's stuck."

Gabby glanced back. The two cars were hurtling toward them. "Here they come." She released her seat belt and quickly climbed over the back of the front seat and prepared to defend them.

"Hang on!" Joel yelled. He punched the accelerator and quickly closed the distance between them and the Scooby van.

The bumpers of the two vehicles crashed together as the Hummer smashed into the back of Scooby van, almost throwing Gabby back into the front seat. The van moved forward, rear wheels spinning, grabbing for traction.

Joel dropped the gear selector into low, engaged his four-wheel drive, and pressed his accelerator to the firewall. All four tires ripped at the earth, throwing grass and dirt in every direction. After several seconds, both vehicles began slowly moving.

The Scooby van inched forward, its rear wheels finally finding some earth to grab and the van ground off the berm of dirt. It picked up speed, slowly at first, then faster and faster as it pounded across the field and finally bounced off the curb and back onto the adjacent pavement.

The Hummer followed, careening onto the pavement and pulling in behind the van.

The two cars pursuing them slammed to a stop, reversed, and accelerated through the field, parallel to the track of their prey, but staying well away from the ditch. They gained on their targets, even though they were bouncing through the rough field. The cars slowly passed the Hummer and Scooby van, accelerating toward an intersecting road.

Half a block ahead of the Hummer and van, the pursuing cars bounced back onto pavement. They turned toward the van and Hummer - dead-heading on a collision course, but they were a little too late. The cars made it to the intersection just as the Hummer passed by. They turned in chase with several Suits leaning out the windows and firing at the Hummer.

Inside the Hummer, a bullet ricocheted off of the rear fender. "Shit!" Joel jerked the wheel to the left, then back to the right.

In the back seat, Gabby, trying to fire out the window, was slung back and forth. "For crying out loud!" She yelled. She finally found a place to brace her feet against the back of the front seat, holding her stable enough to get off a couple of rounds.

BANG! BANG!

The cars behind them slowed, briefly.

Ahead, the Scooby van turned right, down a side street.

"Now where the hell's he going?" Joel shouted. He glanced back and saw the cars were picking up speed again. He didn't follow the Scooby van, but instead went straight.

Behind them, the cars split up, one followed the Scooby van and the other hot on Joel's tail.

Gabby fired again as Joel made a pair of right-hand turns, circling the block.

Intermittent ZINGS announced bullets perforating the Hummer's steel skin. Joel yanked the hummer left and right again, trying to avoid the onslaught from their rear.

"I thought you were a good shot," Joel yelled.

Gabby answered as she was slammed back and forth yet again: "If you'd hold it still for a second, I could..."

A loud pop from the left rear of the Hummer revealed a bullet had found the tire. The Hummer briefly wobbled, then steadied.

Joel patted the steering wheel. "Yeah, baby. Run flat tires. Best invention ever."

Another bullet spidered the rear window of the Hummer.

Gabby crunched down behind the seat and Joel sunk a bit behind the steering wheel.

"Damn it!" Gabby yelled as she popped back up and fired a quick volley out the side window. Sparks flew from the front grill and bumper of their pursuer, briefly slowing them again.

Joel made a hard left. He saw the Scooby van ahead, being chased by the other car, now between them. Joel keyed his radio. "Warren!"

Warren's voice crackled in response: "Kinda' busy here".

"I know," Joel said into the radio. "I'm two behind you. Careful where you shoot. I want you to slow down a little."

"Are you nuts?" Warren responded over the radio.

Joel pulled the radio closer to his lips. "Just do it. Be ready to tap your brakes when I say." Joel stood on the accelerator, closing the distance between the Hummer and the car ahead as the Scooby van slowed. Joel steered into the left side of the road.

Joel yelled back to Gabby: "Get their attention!"

Gabby crawled over to the passenger side of the Hummer, put her gun out the side window and fired off a couple of rounds at the car ahead of them.

Sparks flew from the driver's side of the car.

Joel yelled into the radio: "BRAKES! NOW!"

The brake lights came on at the back of the Scooby van. The pursuing car slammed on their own brakes and Joel nudged his Hummer into the left rear of the pursuit car. The pursuit car violently spun around. Joel pulled his steering wheel to the right, passing the still spinning car.

The spinning car's wheels slammed into a curb. It bounced hard to the side and into a parked pickup truck, then burst into a fireball.

The second car raced through the flames. A pair of flashes from the now lone pursuer proved the chase was still on.

The same round blew out a section of the Hummer's rear window. Gabby and Joel both dove down as Joel continued to slash the Hummer left and right.

"Give me one second of steady, "Gabby said.

"Just say when," Joel answered.

Gabby ejected her empty magazine and shoved a fresh one in. She popped up above the back seat and aimed her pistol through the broken rear window. "NOW!"

Joel centered the steering wheel.

Two bullets zinged through the Hummer's back window and adorned the front windshield with a fresh pair of small, circular vents.

Joel slid low in his seat. "Any time!" he yelled

Joe Gribble

Gabby squeezed off two rounds, a brief second apart.

She watched as sparks decorated the front of the pursuing car, followed by billowing steam. The left front tire exploded and the car careened to the right, bounced up the curb and impaled itself into the corner of a building. Gabby holstered her pistol, retrieved her empty magazine and climbed back over the seat.

Joel turned left, following the Scooby van as it headed back toward town.

Gabby keyed her radio. "You guys okay?"

"Yeah, we're fine," Trish replied over the radio. "Where to?"

"My place is out," Gabby said. "Joel's and Warren's places are out, too - they'll have your tags from surveillance cameras."

"Oh... shit!!!" Joel said to Gabby. "The cops will be all over my condo."

After a brief pause Trish came back over the radio. "Warren says his place is okay. If they get his tags, they'll end up raiding the mayor's house. Department of Motor Vehicles server was a piece of cake."

"Okay," Gabby replied. "We'll split up - meet you there."

"WILCO," Trish said over the radio.

The radio went silent. Gabby turned to Joel: "You better stay off the main drags, your license plate is in the back seat, not to mention your Hummer is shot all to hell."

"Yeah, I noticed," Joel said as he tried to adjust his rear-view mirror. It fell off in his hand. He turned down a side street.

Joel drove past a couple of frat houses in the college ghetto. Even this late at night, several parties were spilling out into the front yards. "I don't understand how anyone could live here."

"Warren's hard core," Gabby answered, "but this is more his vibe. Plus, he can walk to work at the University data center."

"I'm going to park down the block. Just in case," Joel said.

"Good idea."

Joel pulled to the curb. He and Gabby got out, wrapping jackets over their vests.

They walked past a couple of two-story houses, both dark and quiet, then up to Warren's front door, also a two-story.

Gabby stepped through the front door. A loud CRASH came from up the stairs that were right in front of the entrance. She glanced up to see Trish disappear through a bedroom door, carrying one end of the big box that contained the voting machine.

"Careful!" she heard Warren say from inside the upstairs bedroom.

"Sorry," Trish replied. "There aren't any handles on this end of the box."

Gabby started up the stairs.

Joel, came into the house right behind her, but he stopped at the front door. He looked back outside, up and down the block, before coming in and locking the door behind him. He headed for the kitchen.

Gabby stepped into the upstairs bedroom where Trish and Warren had taken the voting machine. In the past, she had heard Warren brag about his 'Lair', but wasn't quite prepared for what she saw. The bedroom wasn't a bedroom. The room was clean, polished, a few computers neatly arranged in a custom-built cabinet against one wall. A nice, albeit small, meeting table held a laptop. There was even a small presentation screen on the wall opposite the computers.

Warren hunkered over the laptop. He handed Trish a cable, already connected to his computer, and she plugged it into the back of the voting machine.

Joel stepped in, carrying a soda from the fridge. "Woah! This is nice. Helluva' lot better than your basement."

Warren answered without looking up: "The basement's where the work gets done." He looked up briefly, waved his arm around the room. "This fluff is for the paying customers."

"The machine won't fit down the basement stairs, so we brought it up here," Trish said.

Gabby sat at a small table nearby, re-loading her magazines from a box of shells.

53

Warren's fingers flew over the keyboard. "Okay, let's see what we have." He looked over at Trish. "Power it up."

Trish plugged the voting machine's power cable into a wall outlet. The machine's lights flickered to life.

A 'STAND BY' graphic marched across the voting machine's screen, regenerating itself and repeating the march several times. After a few seconds it was replaced by instructions to insert a voting card.

Warren hit a few more keys, then data streamed across his laptop's screen. He went to a nearby desktop and started hammering out commands on that computer. "We're in."

The same crew manned the network operations center. One of the operators looked up, startled. He yelled back at the supervisor: "We've got a call home. Rogue machine, same area as the original network penetration."

The supervisor stood and gave his orders to the entire room of operators. "Track it down. I want a location. Don't let it get away this time!" He sat back down and grabbed the phone out of the red box. Punched '6'.

Warren's phone buzzed with a text from Darek: *Run a firmware dump*. "Yeah, yeah. No shit," Warren said to no one in particular. He jammed the commands into his computer, then sat back in his chair as streams of data rapidly filled his screen.

"That's all there is to it?" Joel asked.

"I'm only downloading the code from the firmware," Warren explained. "Figuring out what the code does? That's where the work comes in. Darek's the jock there."

"Figures," Joel said. He pulled Gabby off to the side. "You still trust Darek?" he whispered.

Gabby paused a moment before replying. "Yeah." After another moment of thought she amended her statement. "At least I think so."

"He started all this shit," Joel reminded her, "but we haven't seen him hang his neck out even once. We don't even know where he is."

"He's been with us, somehow," she countered. "Warned us every time the Suits were closing in."

"Yeah, but he's never been at risk," Joel said. "The way I see it, when this goes to hell, you and I, even Trish and Warren, we all go to jail. Darek? No one even knows he's involved."

"What do you mean when this all goes to hell?" Gabby asked.

"Yeah. When. I don't think it's a matter of if."

"I'm loving your positive attitude," Gabby said

Warren's phone buzzed with another text. Trish picked it up. "It's Darek. He says to check the outbound stream."

"Oh shit." Warren hurried back to his desktop computer and pounded out some commands. He followed the output with his finger. "I wasn't expecting that. Not good."

Gabby and Joel stopped their private conversation and stepped closer to the computers.

"What?" Gabby asked.

Warren reached over and quickly yanked the laptop's internet cable out of the computer.

"What?" Joel repeated Gabby's question.

"Damned thing 'E. T'd,'" Warren said.

"'E.T.'d'? What the hell is an 'E.T'?" Gabby asked.

"Phoned home." Warren pointed at a line of code. An IP address flashed on the screen. They have our network address. If they're any good they already know where we are."

"We better work fast," Trish said as she sat down at the desktop computer.

"How long do you need?" Gabby asked.

Warren checked a countdown bar on the laptop. "Maybe fifteen minutes."

Gabby ran out the door and down the stairs, Joel hot on her heels.

"We need warning," Gabby ordered. "And a good egress route. Maybe two."

At the bottom of the stairs, Gabby took up a position near the front window.

Joel headed to the back of the house.

Gabby shut off the interior light, leaving the outside porch light on. She glanced back and saw the light in the rear of the house go out as well. Her radio squawked.

"I have a pretty good view of the back. Good egress out the rear if it's not compromised when they get here." Joel said over the radio.

"Same here," Gabby replied. "I expect they'll dismount up the street. Come in on foot. Front and rear."

"Agree," Joel said over the radio. *"Listen, once Darek finds what's in the code, assuming there is anything, we really need to consider going to the police."*

Gabby spotted movement up the street, a shadow passed beneath a street light. "I may have something."

The shadow solidified briefly, then disappeared again.

Gabby yelled up the stairs: "We have company. How long?"

Warren yelled back down: "Ten minutes."

Upstairs, Warren grabbed his phone and quickly keyed in a number. It only rang once before he heard *"Hello."* "Tyler? You on duty?" Warren asked.

Warren checked the download status. Eight minutes.

"Yeah, two more hours of this boredom," Tyler replied.

"Great. I may need some help," Warren said.

Downstairs, Gabby diligently scanned the outside, careful not to expose herself.

A muffled POP and the outside light shattered. Glass fragments crinkled on the concrete sidewalk. Darkness.

Gabby whispered into the radio: "They're here. Light just went out."

"Dark back here, too," Joel replied.

The window next to Gabby shattered. A small object flew through and landed on the floor. Gabby dove behind a chair as she yelled: "Flash-bang!"

Gabby closed her eyes tightly and crushed her hands against her ears.

BOOM - Thunder and lightning all at once. A second explosion erupted in the back room.

Gabby jumped up from behind the chair. Through a light smoke she saw Joel stagger in from the back, hands over his ears.

Behind Joel, a man in a suit lifted his pistol to swing it down.

Gabby fired twice, hitting the man both times.

The Suit fell on Joel, knocking him to the floor and laying on top of him.

The front door crashed open. Two more Suits rushed inside.

Gabby spun, swinging her pistol around, but not nearly fast enough.

The first Suit already had his gun leveled at Gabby when...

BANG BANG, from the top of the stairwell. Trish.

The first Suit went down. The second Suit re-directed his weapon to the new threat.

At the top of the stairs, Trish dove back behind the wall.

The second Suit through the front door cut loose, pouring shot after shot at the top of the stairs.

Upstairs, bullets from the second Suit pierced the wall and peppered the interior of the room. Warren dove away from the onslaught as large, black gashes appeared in the skin of the voting machine.

Downstairs, Gabby had the new shooter in her sights. BANG BANG and he went down on top of the first gunman.

Near Joel, yet another Suit rushed in from the back room. He brought his gun up to fire at Gabby. Joel fought out from underneath the Suit that fell on him and kicked out, catching the inside of the gunman's knee.

The Suit screamed in agony as his knee popped completely out of its socket. He still tried to fire off a round, but it went wide as he fell to the floor.

Joel jumped on the Suit. He grabbed the Suit's hand to try and wrestle the gun away.

Gabby stood quickly to help, but the second Suit at the front door rolled up from where he had fallen and fired again toward her. She dropped back behind the chair as the wall behind her splintered.

Gabby raised her pistol over the top of the chair, blindly fired in the direction of the front door.

BOOM, BOOM from the top of the stairs permanently ended the threat near the front door. Trish started down, slowly, her gun trained on the two bodies at the foot of the stairs.

Gabby stood cautiously. She pointed her gun at the two men fighting near the back room.

The Suit still had a good grip on his pistol. He saw Gabby as he struggled with Joel, twisted his pistol in her direction. BANG.

The single shot went wide, but forced Gabby back behind the chair.

Almost halfway down the stairs, Trish pivoted toward Joel and his aggressor.

The Suit twisted his wrist to point the gun at Joel's chest. Point Blank.

BOOM. The recoil pushed Trish's gun up, she let it ride up until it safely pointed at the ceiling. 'Joel?" she yelled.

Gabby jumped up from behind the chair. "Joel!" She stepped toward the two bodies piled on the ground. "Joel?"

The body of the Suit moved, slowly at first, then more quickly as Joel pushed the lifeless man off of him. Joel stared at the round circle just off center in the Suit's forehead. He climbed to his feet and looked back at Trish, still standing on the stairs. "You could have killed me!"

Trish smiled. "You're welcome."

Gabby scanned the scene, pistol still ready. "Everyone okay? Joel?"

Joel picked his gun up off the ground. "Yeah, yeah. Flashbang disoriented me."

"Figures," Trish said as she headed back upstairs.

Gabby ejected her magazine and inserted a fresh one. "I hope that's all of them."

All the lights in the house went out.

"SHIT!" Warren yelled from upstairs.

A fusillade of bullets splintered through the front of the house, moving from left to right.

Joel and Gabby dove for the floor.

Outside, a pair of Suits slowly marched toward the front of the apartment, firing automatic rifles as they advanced.

Up the street, red and blue flashing lights, accompanied by sirens, proclaimed the approach of law enforcement.

The Suits quickly retreated into the shadows.

Three vehicles - Campus police - slowed to a stop nearby.

Inside the dark house, Gabby glanced out the front window. "We gotta' go. Cops are here."

Warren and Trish bounded down the stairs, Warren carrying his laptop under his arm. "Campus cops. It's Tyler, he's a friend."

"I don't care how good of a friend he is," Gabby said, "we've got four dead here – if we stay, we'll be in the real cops' hands inside of half an hour."

Warren paused, then nodded his head toward the back of the house. "The van's in the garage.'

They silently filed out the back door, carefully checking for threats as they moved.

Once outside, they crept toward a small row of one-car garages along the alley. Each garage had a small personnel door on the side closest to the houses.

Warren cautiously opened the door, and ushered everyone inside.

"Trish, you drive," Warren said. "I'll open the garage door by hand - no lights."

Warren pulled down on a cord, then raised the big door as quietly as he could.

Once the door was fully open, he climbed into the passenger side of the van, still carrying the laptop under his arm.

Joel and Gabby climbed into the back, quietly closing the van's sliding door.

"Everyone ready?" Trish asked.

"Yeah, let's go," Warren said

Trish started the van. She kept the lights off and backed out of the garage, then drove slowly up the alleyway. At the street, she turned away from the houses and drove, slowly, quietly, in the dark.

"Any chance the download finished?" Gabby asked.

"It was close," Warren said. "There was only about a minute left when the power went out. I'm hoping the laptop might have cached the rest of the data."

Warren flipped open his laptop and hit the power button. Nothing. He poked the button again. Still nothing. He flipped the machine over in his lap and saw a gouge that started about the middle of the back of the laptop and ended at the very edge, getting deeper as it went.

"Fuck. Laptop took a hit," Warren said. He lifted it up and showed the Gabby and Joel in the back seat.

"We're screwed," Joel said.

Trish turned onto a bigger road and flipped the lights on. "We'll go back after the cops leave and get the voting machine."

"We left some dead bodies," Gabby said. "I doubt the Suits had time to police up their dead. Cops will be there for days. They're probably after Warren already."

"Don't worry about me," Warren said. "I tend not to leave fingerprints. Either way the voting machine is dead. The Suits shot it."

"Then we're really screwed, now," Joel said. "No one will believe us. We can't get another voting machine from the warehouse. The Suits probably already moved them anyway."

Gabby's phone rang. "It's Darek." She answered and held the phone up for everyone to hear: "We're all here. You're on speaker."

"The tabulation is definitely being manipulated," Darek said over the phone. *"They pick who they want to win, then sway the count that direction."*

"How the hell are they doing that?" Joel asked.

"It's easy. The hard part is telling the machines who's supposed to win, and by how much."

"You saw the code has an 'input/output' to the power circuit?" Warren asked.

"Yeah, but how does that even work? I'll need the rest of the code to try and figure it out. The only machine we can get to now is the one in the software test office," Darek said.

"I didn't think about that," Gabby said. "The test environment is connected to an actual voting machine. We can use that one.

"Are you nuts?" Joel asked. "There was a gun fight there, too. Cops. Suits. Still all over the building."

"It's Sunday," Gabby said. "They probably just locked the place up 'til Monday. Won't hurt to check."

"What's the address?" Trish asked.

The small jet's engines were still spinning down, engine pitch dropping when the small air-stair flipped down from the plane.

A man in a suit jogged toward the jet, holding a small umbrella to ward off the light drizzle.

Andre hopped down the steps as the Suit arrived to hold the umbrella over Andre's head. Without looking, Andre grabbed the umbrella stem and yanked it out of the man's hand, violently flinging it away. Andre rapidly strode to the waiting stretch SUV. The umbrella bearer lagged several steps behind.

At the waiting SUV another man in a suit held the rear door open and Andre climbed inside.

Andre settled back into the seat and lit a cigarette. The light of the flame illuminated another man, wearing a suit of course, sitting in the back.

Andre's door closed and umbrella man climbed into the driver's seat.

"Where are they, Raul?" Andre asked

"We're not sure, sir" the man in the back answered.

Andre took a drag on his cigarette. "We don't pay you to be 'not sure'." He handed a slip of paper over the seat to the driver, then turned his attention back to Raul. "They still need a voting machine. There's only one left that they can get to."

The SUV rapidly pulled away, a small caravan of two other cars followed in tight formation.

"How long?" Andre asked the driver.

"Twenty minutes, sir," the driver replied.

"Make it fifteen," Andre ordered.

The SUV lurched forward.

"You still want her captured alive?" Raul asked.

Andre pulled his pistol from his shoulder holster. He checked it, then chambered a round and put it back in his holster.

Raul nodded. He pulled his own pistol and chambered a round himself.

The Scooby van, lights extinguished, rolled to a stop half a block from the State Department's office building.

Inside the van, Trish shifted into park and killed the engine. Everyone peered through the windshield at the building where Gabby had gotten into the first fight with the Suits.

"See anything?" Gabby asked from the back seat.

"No cars. No people. Just some police tape," Warren said as he peered through a pair of binoculars.

"That's an ambush if I ever saw one," Joel said.

"Maybe,' Gabby said as she quietly eased her door open. "Only one way to find out."

The rest of the team followed Gabby as she silently moved closer to the building. She waved Joel and Trish on, while she and Warren took cover behind a bush near the building.

"Does your test machine connect to the internet?" Warren asked quietly.

"Yeah," Gabby answered.

Warren frowned. "Okay. We'll have to kill that connection first thing, or they'll be onto us."

"Then how will we get the data to Darek?"

Warren held up a USB thumb drive. "Easy. Old school."

They both startled as Trish and Joel, bent low, came around the bush and joined them.

"No one. Not even a car nearby," Trish said.

"I still say it's a trap," Joel said.

"Maybe," Gabby said, "but we don't have a choice."

Gabby pulled out her pistol and checked that she had a round chambered. "Trish, you and Joel stand security. I'll take Warren up to the second floor."

The rest of the team pulled out their weapons. They crouched low and headed, single file, toward the building.

They stopped at a utility box near a side door, labeled "LASER SECURITY".

The rest of the team provided lookout as Warren felt around the edge of the box's door. He took a jumper wire out of his backpack and attached it. Next, he used a screwdriver to punch out the lock, then slowly opened the door. The attached jumper wire stretched out to keep the box intrusion alarm from sounding. Inside, several bundles of wires led to various parts of the building.

Warren pulled a small electronic device from his backpack, and connected the tone generator to a pair of wires. He tracked the wiring by moving the connector from one wire to the next.

'Any chance you can get this done sometime tonight?" Joel asked.

"Patience, my friend. Patience," Warren said.

Warren attached another pair of jumpers across some wires, then slowly closed the box door and removed the external jumper. "We should be good."

"Should be?" Joel asked.

Warren shrugged. "Not my chosen profession. More of a hobby. Warren moved to the side door. He pulled out a set of lock picks and quickly worked the lock. He held his breath and slowly turned the knob, then gently pushed the door open. He exhaled. "No alarm."

The team moved quickly inside.

Once inside the hallway, the only illumination came from the emergency exit signs, but it was enough to keep them from falling over each other.

Last in, Gabby pulled the door closed behind her. She stepped past the others. "This way," her voice echoed inside the cramped hallway. She led them to the end of the hallway, then paused before quickly sticking her head into the next hallway, checking both left and right, then pulling her head back. "We're good." Trish, you go right. Front entrance is that way. Joel, you go left and watch the loading dock. I'll take Warren upstairs to the test room."

Outside, three cars slowed to a stop down the street, near the Scooby van.

Four men emerged from each car, all wearing suits. Most of the Suits were carrying compact, automatic rifles. They deferred to Andre, who led them toward the building. He pulled his pistol and waved it toward the van.

Two men detoured from the group, weapons at the ready. They checked out the Scooby van as the others headed toward the building.

Without words, Andre pointed at one group, then the front of the building. He indicated the rest were to follow him and he headed toward the back of the structure.

Inside the building, the front lobby was well lit. Trish, mostly hidden beside the corner of a wall, had a good view of the front door and the glass panels on either side of it. She quietly spoke into her radio: "In position."

Joel heard Trish state her status as he entered a large room at the back of the building. One large garage door and a small personnel door were at the back wall, both closed. He walked over to them to make sure they were locked. He sat down in a chair behind a small desk, littered with paperwork. He whispered into his radio: "I've got the back."

"Copy," Gabby said as she led Warren quickly up the stairs. She stopped at the landing, eased the door open and glanced into the hallway. Seeing nothing, she motioned for Warren to follow her through the door.

Warren tailed Gabby as she moved quickly past the break room and turned down the hallway leading to the test room. They moved cautiously, stepping over, and ducking under, several bands of police tape.

Gabby tried the handle when they reached the test office door. Locked. She reached into her backpack and retrieved her swipe card. She swiped it through the sensor and pushed the door again. No luck.

"Back up," Warren said, quietly.

Gabby stepped back.

Warren raised the butt of his pistol and swung it hard, shattering the glass in the upper half of the door. He reached inside and twisted the knob to open the door.

"Shit, Warren," Gabby said. "That's bound to set off the alarm."

Warren pushed the door open and stepped inside the testing office, crunching on broken glass. He examined the edge of the door jamb. "This door isn't wired. We're good."

"Dammit," Gabby said, following him inside. "You didn't know that." She pointed at her desk. "This is mine." She bent over and typed a few keystrokes.

The password box popped up and she typed in her code.

She stepped back and Warren sat down. He pulled the USB thumb drive out of his pocket.

"*I may have something*," Trish said over the radio.

Out front, Trish scanned the large windows that made up the front wall. She saw another movement in the darkness beyond the glass. She shifted position so she had a better view. Beyond the glass, a man in a suit briefly stepped into the light from the lobby.

Trish keyed her mike: "They're here."

Trish was focused on the front door when one of the side wall windows burst inward, glass shards knifing through the air. She moved back behind the wall just as a blinding flash and loud explosion erupted in the lobby. Trish keyed her mike again: "A little help?"

She stepped around the edge of the wall as two men leapt into the building through the busted window. Trish leveled her pistol and fired twice.

The Suit on the left went down hard, but the Suit on the right fired a burst in her direction as he dove out of the way.

Trish quickly retreated behind the rapidly splintering wall.

In the back, Joel heard Trish's request for help. He jumped to his feet and raced into the hallway. He keyed his radio on the run. "On my way."

In the test office, Warren held the USB thumb drive near the computer port, when they heard Joel over their radios. Warren stabbed the flash drive into the USB slot on the computer then hammered away at the keyboard.

Gabby pulled her weapon. "Keep at it. Let me know when you've got the code downloaded." She crouched, moving toward the door.

Warren continued to pound away at the keys. After a short moment a download timeline popped up on his screen. *Seems like we've been here before,* Warren told himself. He pulled his sidearm and moved to the door, crouching as Gabby had. He joined her at the door where Gabby was checking the hallway.

She looked back at Warren.

"About five minutes," Warren said, anticipating her question.

Gabby glanced out the door, up and down the hallway. All clear. She whispered to Warren. "I'm going up to the hallway intersection. You stay here and monitor the download."

A small, muffled explosion rumbled beneath their feet.

"That came from the back of the building," Warren said.

"Keep your eyes open," Gabby said as she scrambled down the hallway.

In the back of the building, the door knob in the personnel door knob flew out of the door and impaled the chair where Joel had been sitting minutes earlier. The door quickly opened and two men in suits entered, weapons drawn, scanning the room.

Andre followed them in, with yet another Suit covering his back.

Andre motioned for the men to advance. They moved rapidly, but methodically, into the hallway.

Joel arrived at the front of the building and cautiously approached. It was quiet, but the smell of gunpowder hung heavy in the air. He spotted Trish, still posted behind the edge of the wall on the other side of the hallway. He crouched low and stepped into the hall.

BOOM. BOOM.

The shots came from behind the guard desk, splintering the wall near Joel. He quickly backed up.

Trish signaled him, holding up two fingers, then pointing to the guard desk.

Joel glanced into the hallway just as a rifle poked up from behind the guard post. Two short automatic bursts and the ceiling lights shattered. The only remaining light was from the emergency exit signs. He checked around the corner of the wall again, focused on the guard desk. He saw movement in the shadows. Two Suits– one deploying right, the other left.

Joel and Trish. no longer exposed by the lights, stepped into the hallway, moving forward.

They split in opposite directions, each heading for one of the Suits.

A loud bang outside diverted their attention. They glanced toward the shattered window and saw a black gloved hand flash forward, tossing something inside.

Joel and Trish both dove back as the flash-bang detonated.

Concussed by the unexpected explosion, Joel and Trish heard a single shot - BOOM - followed by a long stream of automatic fire. Drywall and splinters of wood cascaded around them.

"AHHH," Trish groaned through gritted teeth, grabbing her leg.

Joel stood and saw a dark figure quickly move into the room through the shattered window. Joel fired several rounds toward the origin of the automatic rifle fire. BOOM. BOOM. BOOM. He dropped back down, grabbed the shoulder strap of Trish's vest and dragged her back to the hallway.

BOOM. Another round came from the front, then quiet.

Joel ignored the noise and pulled Trish back toward safety. An open office door invited them in. Once inside, Joel checked Trish's wound. "Not too bad, bone's in one piece."

From one of the pockets on his vest, he pulled a first aid envelope. He snapped it back and forth, then ripped the envelope open and removed a green rag. He wrapped it tightly around her leg. "Hold it tight. Should stop the bleeding."

Trish grimaced, but held the bandage on her leg. "Got it. I don't think I can walk, though. Did you see that guy?"

"What guy?" Joel asked as he checked her pulse.

"Not sure. Someone. In black. Not one of the Suits."

Joel shook his head. "Didn't see anyone." He re-loaded a fresh magazine and stepped toward the door. He glanced out just as Gabby called over the radio.

"What the hell's going on down there," Gabby asked.

Joel checked the hallway again and keyed his mike" "Threat's eliminated. I think. Trish is hit."

Upstairs, Warren heard Joel's radio call. He jumped to his feet. "How bad?" he asked into his radio. He drew his pistol and moved toward the door, abandoning the post he was assigned.

In the first floor hallway, Andre followed two of the Suits into a stairwell, heading up. The fourth followed them, providing rear cover.

Gabby left the break room and headed down the hallway toward the stairs. "Stay with the computer," she ordered Warren over the radio. "I'll give Joel and Trish a hand." She turned a corner, bent low, her weapon ready.

Ahead, two Suits crept out of the stairway door.

Gabby spotted them and retreated back into the break room.

Andre and the final Suit emerged, unseen by Gabby, from the stairwell.

Gabby moved further back into the break room. She positioned herself where she could still see the hallway and remain hidden. She pulled off her backpack and put it on the floor.

She watched as the two lead Suits passed by, slowly, quietly. Gabby keyed her radio and warned Warren, barely louder than a whisper: "Warren, two headed your way."

Warren was almost to the door when he got Gabby's message. He retreated back into the testing room.

In the hallway, Andre heard Gabby's radio squelch when she unkeyed the mike. He looked over toward the break room, then held up his hand. The Suit behind him stopped and reversed to cover Andre's six.

Gabby moved toward the partially open door to attack the two Suits she saw heading toward Warren. She stopped short of the door, something in her spine telling her there were others nearby.

Andre spotted Gabby's shadow as it spilled through the door opening. He stood quickly and kicked the door inward.

The door hit Gabby hard and she fell backward.

Andre leaped into the room and fired. BOOM. BOOM.

Gabby rolled behind a counter. She blindly fired over the top.

Andre moved to the side, continuing to fire.

In the hallway, the Suit providing rear guard slowly walked backward, covering Andre's rear. When the Suit heard Andre kick in the door, he spun around, leveled his automatic rifle, and ran toward the break room.

In the stairwell, Joel heard the shots. He rushed up the stairs, taking them three at a time. He crashed through the door into the second-floor hallway.

Just ahead Joel saw another Suit.

The Suit heard Joel behind him. He spun around, fired a burst from the automatic, spraying bullets into the wall, across the stairwell door, then onto the other wall.

Joel dove down to avoid the onslaught of lead. He fired from a crouch, hitting the Suit in the arm and sending his rifle flying.

Joel jumped up and ran directly toward the Suit.

The Suit was still standing, and he grabbed for a knife in a scabbard on his shoulder holster.

Joel levelled his pistol and fired on the run. BOOM.. click... click.

The round missed the wounded Suit.

Joel knew he was racing toward the sharp steel of an edged weapon. He didn't slow, tossing his pistol away and when almost to the Suit he went into a slide, one leg raised and aimed at the Suit's knee.

The Suit dodged to the side.

Joel snapped his foot up, attempting to kick the Suit in the crotch. The kick missed, having only a muted effect on the Suit.

The Suit slashed down with his knife, finding its mark in Joel's shoulder.

Joel's vest deflected the brunt of the attack, but the knife did find some meat. Blood immediately stained Joel's shirt. "UNHHH!!" Joel exhaled at the pain. He grabbed the Suit in an arm bar, holding the knife at bay.

The Suit swapped hands with the knife. Holding it in his wounded arm he slashed at Joel's throat.

Joel dodged, kicked again - this time landing squarely in the Suit's groin. Joel pulled the Suit down, and they erupted in a ball of wounded, frenzied fury. The Suit continuously thrusted at Joel, and Joel struggled to parry each attack.

In the testing room, Warren could hear the commotion out in the hall. He backed up and took a hidden position behind a pillar. Looking around the edge of the pillar and through the windows into the hall, he saw two Suits maneuvering for attack. They stopped close to the door and split up, one on each side of the door. One of the Suits raised his foot to kick in the door.

Warren quickly slid his gun outside the pillar and fired. BOOM.

Glass from one of the windows shattered all around the door.

The Suits backed up a step and both let loose with their automatic weapons, blowing out the remaining windows and unleashing a hail of lead into the software testing room.

Warren tried to make himself small behind the concrete pillar, eyes shut as the lead gnawed at everything around him.

Both automatic weapons went silent at the same time.

Warren glanced back out into the hallway. He saw the Suits ejecting magazines and reaching for fresh loads. He spun around from behind the pillar and fired quickly. BOOM. BOOM. Both of his shots went wide, and he braced himself for the worst. That's when he saw it. A dagger flew from somewhere on the left and pierced the neck of the Suit on that side. The Suit grabbed at his neck and went down.

The other Suit got a fresh magazine loaded and spun in the direction of the new threat. He raised his rifle.

Warren fired off another round, again missing the Suit. The Suit dove down below the window.

Warren retreated back behind the pillar, eyes clenched shut, waiting for the expected onslaught.

Nothing. He looked back around the pillar. Saw nothing. Heard nothing. He carefully stepped toward the window, grimacing when he stepped on crinkly, broken glass. With one quick motion, he took the last step to the window sill and quickly looked over it, pistol ready.

The second Suit lay crumpled on the floor, another victim of a knife attack.

Warren slowly pulled back, then went out the door and headed toward the break room.

Inside the break room, Gabby crouched behind a cabinet as rounds hammered into it, some bouncing off, but others thundered through, splintering the wood cabinets behind her.

During a pause, she raised her pistol above the counter and blindly fired her last two rounds in the direction of the onslaught, then dropped back behind her shelter. Another fusillade slammed into the other side of the counter.

She curled up into a tight ball, until she heard the other gun go dry. She leaped up, dropped her gun and scrambled over the counter toward Andre.

Gabby covered the short distance between them and launched into Andre with a pair of punches.

Andre was ready. Coolly, he fended off her jabs and responded with a backhand that caught Gabby across the face. She staggered backwards.

Andre stood upright, placing his pistol on a nearby table. He straightened his suit then slowly walked toward Gabby.

Gabby put her fists up, not backing away, her face already beginning to swell.

She jabbed at Andre. He easily parried her shots.

She punched again. Still no joy.

A slight grin formed on Andre's face. He shifted his stance, preparing for attack.

Andre lashed out with a right-hand jab.

Gabby dodged the brunt of the strike, but suffered a glancing blow to her shoulder. Gabby tucked down slightly, then unleashed with a flurry of blows.

Andre was prepared for the onslaught and deflected most of the blows, but a savage kick to the inside of his leg took him to one knee.

Gabby kicked straight at his face, but Andre grabbed her foot before she could connect. She awkwardly stood on one leg while Andre held her other.

Andre slowly pulled her toward him.

Gabby dropped down onto her butt, reaching for a plastic chair. She swung it hard.

The chair shattered across Andre's head, leaving a deep cut on his cheek. He grimaced, loosening his grip on Gabby's leg.

She kicked with her other leg, attempting to break free.

Andre held on, continuing to draw her toward him, his grimace replaced by a sadistic smile.

Gabby continued to kick as she was sucked toward her enemy. She pulled the knife from her vest and stabbed one of Andre's hands.

Andre screamed in pain and released his grip on Gabby.

Gabby scooted backward as fast as she could.

Andre looked at her, scowling. He retrieved his pistol from the table and ejected the magazine.

Gabby glanced at her own empty pistol on the floor nearby as she continued to back pedal. She abruptly stopped when she crashed into her backpack near the wall.

Slowly, methodically, Andre pulled another magazine from his pocket as he stepped toward Gabby.

Gabby glanced at the backpack near her, zipper open. She quickly reached in...

Andre inserted the magazine into his pistol. He jacked a round into the chamber and stopped walking. He slowly raised the pistol, aiming it directly at Gabby.

BOOM.

Andre jerked backward; a startled look fell over his face.

A small hole adorned Gabby's backpack. Smoke curled up from inside.

Gabby pulled her hand out of the backpack, holding the gun she took from the front desk guard the day before.

Andre struggled to lift his gun again, his mouth still open, some blood starting to leak from his lips. A red spot grew on his chest.

BOOM. Gabby fired again.

Andre jerked back once more. He fell to his knees, pistol dropping from his hand. The look of surprise on his face faded to lifelessness. He stared briefly, then fell face first onto the floor.

She heard Warren yell from the hallway: "Gabby?"

"In here," she replied.

Gabby slowly rose to her feet.

Warren rushed in, gun ready. "You okay?"

"Yeah. You?"

"Fine," Warren said. "There's some weird shit going on, though."

Joel rounded the door.

Warren saw him. "Where's Trish?" he asked.

Gabby spotted the blood on Joel's chest. "You're hit." She rushed toward him and pressed her hand on his chest near the wound.

Joel flinched, then took her hand and briefly held it, before pulling it away from his injury. "It's only a cut. I'm okay." He turned to Warren. "Trish is okay. She's holed up in an office downstairs."

Warren keyed his radio. "Trish, I'm coming down." He quickly stepped out into the hallway and ran toward the stairs.

Gabby grabbed her gun and pushed a fresh magazine home. "Let's get the USB drive."

They cautiously walked down the hallway, Gabby leading. Both had their guns ready.

Near the software lab, Gabby stepped over the first dead Suit lying in a large pool of blood. She reached the other, also a bloody mess. She kicked the gun out of the lifeless Suit's reach.

Joel knelt down by the first body and examined the knife sticking out of his neck. "Who the hell brings a knife to a gunfight?"

"Knife?" Gabby asked. She dropped down to look at the other dead body. She rolled him over and spotted the steel weapon lodged in his chest. She smiled, then hid her smile and stood back up. "It's not a knife. It's a dagger."

She went inside the software testing lab, Joel following behind her. "Damn," she said. The room was shot all to hell. She stepped across the broken glass to the computer. The computer itself had a large bullet hole in it, and there was no USB drive. "It's gone."

"Well, that's just fuckin' fine," Joel said. "Who the hell could've taken it?"

Gabby's phone chirped. Another text from Darek: *"Cops on the way. Get out."*

Sirens wailed in the distance.

"We better go," Gabby said.

Once outside the building, Warren and Gabby helped Trish walk as they tried to make their escape. Joel provided rear guard.

"So, what next?" Joel asked. "We still don't know where the USB went. Without that we still don't have any proof."

"It's gotta' be whoever knifed those Suits," Warren said.

"Daggers," Joel corrected. "They were daggers."

Gabby glanced back at him.

Joel shrugged.

They reached the Scooby van and helped Trish into the back seat. Warren got into the driver's seat.

Warren stared at the building as he started the engine. "I still don't frickin' get it."

Gabby's phone buzzed. Text from Darek: *"I couldn't figure it out either. That's why I had to come. Tell Warren to look at the roof-line."*

"Darek says to look at the roof-line," Gabby relayed.

Warren shrugged. "Just a couple of satellite dishes."

"There were boxes of those in the warehouse," Joel said.

Warren dropped the van into gear. A big smile crept across his face. "Oh. Yeah. Smart."

"What?" Joel asked

Warren gestured toward the satellite dishes "They're communicating with the voting machines using those sat receivers. It's genius." He turned down a side road and headed back toward town.

"We've been over this. They're not connected to the voting machines," Joel said.

"Not directly," Warren said. "They're communicating through the power lines within the building. It's a system. It's all downstream of the power transformers, so... Easy."

"Holy shit!" Joel said. "I get it. It's genius."

Gabby's phone buzzed again. "It's Darek. He says Joel and I are to meet some friends of his at Fountain Square."

"What about Trish?" Joel asked.

"She needs a doctor," Warren said. "I know a place where the docs don't talk, down in Kentucky."

It was almost four a.m. when the Scooby van pulled to a stop near two large, blacked out SUVs parked at Fountain Square. Several men stood nearby.

Gabby and Joel stepped out of the Scooby van.

One of the men approached them.

"I'm Special Agent Knowles. Are you Ms. Hernandez?"

"Maybe," Gabby said, closely eyeing the man.

"You're needed in Washington," Knowles said. "We're here to escort you."

Gabby stepped back. "How do I know..." Her phone buzzed with another text from Darek: *"They're okay. Go with them. It's important."*

Gabby shrugged. She showed Joel the text.

"I'm not letting you go alone," Joel said.

Gabby nodded, then turned to Knowles. "Let's go."

Knowles held out his hand. "You won't need your guns. We're your security."

Gabby looked at him suspiciously. "I think we'll keep our weapons." She stepped past Knowles and headed to the first van.

Joel stepped to follow Gabby, but Knowles stopped him.

Knowles looked at the blood on Joel's shirt, pulled Joel's jacket back to see the extent of the injury. He waved at another man: "Pat, take a look at this wound.

Joel resisted, tried to back away from Knowles. "Easy Mr. Baxter. Pat's a medic. He'll take care of you."

Gabby and Joel followed their escorts into the Senate Hearing Room.

Gabby wrung her hands, nervously.

Joel smiled, totally relaxed.

Their escort pointed to a pair of seats right up in front of the huge dais.

The room was mostly empty of people, save the various senators and a few aides. The senators were generally mingling with each other up at the dais, not paying much attention to the witnesses who just walked in.

Senator Evelyn Harriet, early 50s, entered and made her way, most businesslike, to her seat near the center of the dais. She looked out and smiled at Gabby and Joel, gave them a slight wave.

Senator Black entered and made his way to the center chair. The other senators broke from their conversations and slowly moved to their seats.

Senator Black slammed down the gavel as he sat down. "This meeting will come to order." He harshly looked at Senator Harriet. "This meeting was called by the ranking member, but without any agenda. I'm tempted to cancel the meeting outright, but in our new found sense of bipartisan unity..."

Senator Harriet looked somewhat shocked. "Mister Chairman, I did not call the meeting..."

Black turned to an aide, who handed over a piece of paper. Black studied it quickly. Frowned. He looked over at Senator Harriet as he waved the paper in the air. "According to this, the request for this meeting came from your office, Senator Harriet."

She quickly turned to her own aide and urgently whispered something into her ear.

The aide rushed off, pulling out her phone as she left.

Senator Black watched the aide leave, then took the opportunity to berate the senator from the other party: "You even specified this be a closed hearing. If this is some sort of joke to waste this committee's time..."

Several of the other senators reached to gather their papers. A few stood to leave.

Harriet's jovial expression went stern. "I'd like to call my witness," she said to Senator Black.

Gabby shrunk into her seat. *This is already turning into a shit show. Thanks Darek.*

Joel leaned forward, grinning ear to ear.

Senator Black tapped the eraser end of his pencil against the desk. He eventually nodded. "Make this quick. Elections are tomorrow and many of us have a lot of work to do before then."

Senator Harriet turned to look at Gabby. Her hard expression turned soft. "Young lady, would you please introduce yourself?"

Gabby glanced at Joel.

He nodded encouragingly, urging her on.

Gabby leaned toward the microphone on the desk before her. "My name is Gabriella Hernandez. I was asked by some government officials to be here. I really have no idea why. Other than..." Gabby paused. She thought better of what she was about to say and leaned back away from the microphone.

"Other than what, dear?" Senator Harriet softly asked.

Joel leaned close to Gabby and whispered in her ear: "Tell them what we found in the machine level code."

Gabby nodded at him. She took a deep breath and leaned back to the microphone. She hesitated, cleared her throat. "I'm a software tester, contracted by the Ohio Department of State to evaluate the Domain voting software."

Senator Harriet looked over at Senator Black, an insincere smile pasted across her lips. "I believe Senator Black instituted this program across each state? Very important for our elections tomorrow."

Senator Black hesitantly nodded.

Gabby cleared her throat again: "We found some...Irregularities in the algo."

Senator Black leaned forward, glaring at Gabby.

"Algo?" Senator Harriet asked. "I'm sorry, what is that, Miss Hernandez?"

"I'm sorry, Senator, "Gabby replied. "Algorithm. We found that while the Domain tabulation software is fine, there is malicious code embedded directly into the voting machine chips."

Senator Black's face turned a crimson red as he listened to Gabby's testimony.

"It allows someone," Gabby continued, "I don't know who, to feed incorrect information to the tabulation software. It changes the vote count."

Senator Black exploded. "This is ridiculous. This witness has not been vetted. Just more of the wholly disproved stolen election conspiracy nonsense."

Black slammed down his gavel. "This meeting is adjourned."

Joel stood up. "We have valuable information this committee needs to hear. The whole nation needs to hear."

Black stood, pointed the gavel at Joel. "You're out of line, boy." Black pointed to the back of the room. "Sergeant-at-arms. Escort these two from the chamber immediately."

A large monitor near the side of the hearing room glowed on. Everyone looked in that direction.

"What the hell is this?" Senator Black asked/

He picked up a remote control by his side and repeatedly pushed a button.

The monitor stayed lit and an image slowly came into focus.

Black pushed the button harder. More aggressively. Nothing. He threw it down and waved at an aide. "Unplug that damned thing!"

The image came into focus. It was a visual of a well appointed office, and the name plate on the desk clearly identified the owner as Buck Winston. Senator Black and another man sat across from Winston's desk.

The aide stopped moving toward the monitor. He looked back at Senator Black.

The audio crackled to life and the video played:

"...*he's getting ready to fix your most glorious fuck-up yet,*" the man behind the desk, Winston, said.

"*What the hell are you talking about?*" Senator Black could be heard saying.

"*The voting certification bullshit. That's what,*" continued Winston.

In the video, Senator Black pulled out a handkerchief and wiped his brow.

Back in the hearing room, sweat dripped down Black's forehead as well. He glanced around.

Everyone in the room stared back at Black.

The Sergeant-at-Arms grabbed both Gabby and Joel, lifting them from their chairs by their arms.

Gabby fought back.

A group of men came running from the back of the room to assist the Sergeant-at-Arms.

Senator Harriet rose from her chair as she yelled: "Sergeant-at-Arms, hands off my witnesses."

The flurry around Gabby and Joel stopped as the playback continued on the monitor:

"*After that last fiasco of an election,*" Senator Black's voice emanated from the speakers, "*the people needed to be able to trust the process.*"

"*And your dumb ass thought a public test of the software would do that?* Buck shook his head. "*We were fine. Now I've got to clean up your shit.*"

Senator Black jumped up from behind the dais and pointed at the monitor. "Turn that off. This is fake. How is that even playing. This is a closed hearing. Turn it off!"

No one moved, not even Black's staffer.

Black jumped from around the table and tried to make his way to the monitor. Several senators blatantly impeded his progress.

The picture in the video faded to a round conference table. The video moved in close and focused on a man sitting in one of the table's chairs. The man wore an obvious disguise - a white wig, face mask that looked like an old man, and an old-fashioned robe. He held a large staff, even as he was seated.

Senator Black still tried to fight his way, unsuccessfully, toward the monitor. Even his own party members now impeded his progress.

"You don't know me...." the man on the monitor began.

Gabby recognized the voice. She smiled, exhaled in relief.

"... and you never will," the man continued. "You can call me Merlin." There was a short pause as Merlin leaned slightly forward. "What you should know is this.... There are forces attempting to undermine our democracy. And they live among us."

Merlin's face faded from the screen, replaced by a series of still photos of well-known politicians and businessmen.

Merlin continued to talk as the images played over the screen. "A cabal of international businessmen and politicians have modified the code inside the chips of voting machines. Almost untraceable. They now determine who wins, and who loses, in every election."

The last photo that came into view stayed on the screen. Senator Black. The photo grew to fill the entire monitor.

Even Senator Black stopped struggling to get to the monitor. He looked around - all eyes were on him now.

The still photo stream faded back to Buck Winston's office and the video resumed.

"Some hacker broke in," Winston continued. *"Not sure how, but he, she, they? They're good."*

"They won't be able to figure it out, "Senator Black said. *"No way. You have the best on this, right. That's what you said.*

"As soon as you start thinking you can't be beat, you'll lose every time." Winston said.

Black pointed at the other man sitting with them. *"So, he's your backup plan?"*

"We all knew it might come to this," Winston said. *"Eventually. Hell, even you agreed that if we got exposed we'd have to tie up all the loose ends and move to the next phase."*

"The plan was to blame it on the Domino software," Senator Black said.

"No, these guys are too good," Winston said. *"They'll figure that out. We have to deal... with finality."*

Senator Black twisted in his seat. *"Okay. Just do it quickly."* Black looked directly at Andre. *"No fucking witnesses."*

In the hearing room, Senator Black backed away. "Stop this nonsense now. This is all a fake. It's absurd. I'm not going to stand for this."

Senator Harriet motioned to the Sergeant-at-arms: "Please take the Senator into custody."

Senator Black was defiant: "You can't do that, you don't have the authority, God damn it!" He gathered his papers from the dais and motioned for his aides to follow him. "Let's go."

Black's aides stood unmoving, aghast.

The Sergeant-at-Arms moved from Gabby and Joel to Black. His entire team followed. They grabbed Black roughly.

"Hands off me! I'm a United States Senator. You can't do this to me."

Black fought, but to no avail. The sergeant-at-arms and his men carried Black bodily out of the chamber.

The video faded to a graphic: it showed a line drawing of a Greek Goddess, the name **SOTERIA** below it, and beneath the drawing of the goddess was a picture of a knight's helmet emblazoned on top of a staff and a flash of lightning.

Senator Harriet turned to one of her aides. "I want a copy of that video."

The aide rushed out.

Senator Harriet turned to Gabby. "I want to thank you, young lady, for bringing this to our attention."

Harriet stood and turned to leave, but stopped and looked back at Gabby. "Oh, and thank your wizard friend, too. I'm sure we're going to want to talk to him."

Gabby nodded at the Senator. She leaned over to Joel and whispered: "This whole thing will probably die here. Who knows, even Harriet might be in on it." Gabby waved at the people still in the room. "Hell, I bet they're all in on it."

Joel smiled broadly and whispered back: "Won't matter if they are. I'm willing to bet the next round at Clancy's that this video is making the rounds all over the world. Right now."

Joel pulled out his phone, hit a few buttons and smiled again. He showed it to Gabby. The very same video played on Joel's news feed.

The mid-day sun streamed through the massive windows in Buck Winston's office. He stared at his own phone. A stick image of some woman, **SOTERIA**, above a knight's helmet, filled his screen. He shook his head, pocketed his phone and briefly contemplated. He reached out and hit the intercom button on his desk phone.

"Yes sir?" Gwen answered.

"Call my wife," Buck said. "Have her meet me at the hangar. And call the pilot. I want to be wheels up in an hour."

"He'll want a destination," Gwen said.

"Brussels."

Gabby and Joel walked along a boulevard, the capital building behind them.

"So, you okay with Darek now?" Gabby asked.

"Not sure. Not sure at all. I really want to know who's backing him. Who's paying his bills."

Gabby stopped walking. She stared across the boulevard. "Damn."

Joel followed her gaze. "What?" Then he saw it. Across the road, a reflection in a storefront window - Darek. He waved at them.

Gabby took off across the road, dodging traffic as she ran toward the reflection. Joel jumped in behind her.

Joel yelled at her. "Be careful."

Gabby arrived at the window, but there was no one there. She looked around for Darek. Nothing. She noticed a large envelope that sat on the window sill. She walked to it and picked it up, turned it over in her hands. The envelope bore the now familiar image of **Soteria** above their old unit emblem. The envelope also had her name on it.

Joel stumbled up behind her.

"He's gone," Gabby said as she held up the envelope for Joel to see.

Gabby opened the envelope and poured out a greeting card and a passport.

She opened the card and an audio message played:

"Well done, Gabriella," Darek's voice said. "I hope you enjoyed this little adventure. If you did, another one awaits. I've talked to the rest of the team. We want to welcome you to **Soteria**."

She opened the passport and saw her picture. Inside was a visa to Belgium.

"Oh, hell no," Joel said, looking over her shoulder. "No. I'm not okay with you going to Belgium. Definitely not if Darek is involved. And what the hell is this *Soteria* he keeps talking about?"

"I don't know. Maybe a club or something." Gabby reached into the envelope and pulled out another passport. She opened it and looked inside. "It's okay. You're going with me." Gabby handed Joel another passport, then turned and walked down the sidewalk.

Joel followed, hurrying to catch up with Gabby. "What do you? ...No. No we're not. Wait a minute. Slow Down." He opened the passport she had given him. A picture stared back at him. "Hey! How'd he get my passport?"

85

Gabby continued walking down the street, broadly smiling. "Should be fun."

THE END

Joe Gribble is a novelist and award-winning screenwriter. His stories range from mythical, to modern drama, to comedies, to his favorite—action thrillers. He is retired from the US Air Force and has been a technical manager on programs supporting the Army, Navy, and Marine Corps. His characters are drawn from the many people he has worked with, and continues to work with as a volunteer for Team Rubicon (a veteran led disaster response organization).

Other **Novels** by Joe:

Silent Lightning – Putnam
Silent Salvo – Putnam
Hometown Heroes – Amazon
Darkest Edge – Amazon
Archives of Murder – Amazon
Coal Town Murder – Amazon
Merlin's Millennium – Jumpmaster Press

Feature Movie by Joe:
Darkest Edge – Amazon, YouTube, and other streaming services

Made in the USA
Coppell, TX
07 December 2023